SAMANTHA'S RIG

CAROL CHOOMACK

Charleston, SC
www.PalmettoPublishing.com

Samantha's Rig
Copyright © 2022 by Carol Choomack

All rights reserved

Hardcover ISBN: 979-8-8229-0562-7
Paperback ISBN: 979-8-8229-0563-4
eBook ISBN: 979-8-8229-0564-1

PREFACE

This book is the sequel to Behind 'The Glass Door.' 'Samantha's Rig' is a fictional tale that will answer many of the questions you may have had. It tells of Love and the unions of souls. It is woven of friendships, betrayal's, lies and unexpected murder. Many of the characters in this book are real and true friends of mine, who throughout their lives have inspired me in a multitude of ways.

My writing style and the way that I find myself into a story line is unique in that I never have a plan. My mother always told me I had a way of telling stories and she implored me to write books. So, I have taken her good advice and explored the world of writing and publishing. Although she, Lillian (Nicki) Cottone is no longer here on this earth. I call upon her for each word that I write. Somehow, my fingers type away without much thought and in that I know she is ever present.

Although I am not the likes of Nora Roberts or James Patterson to name a few. I have found success because of each and every one of you who have graciously taken the time to explore my words and read my works.

I heartfeltly thank each and every one of you.

Enjoy and many thanks.

Acknowledgements

I thank all of my friends, especially Jan Cree, Leslie Kachadoorian and Dr. Maryann D'Ambrosio, for your kind patience and encouragement during this new journey. Your support has been encouraging and I am ever grateful.

Samantha's Rig tells of life's strife and the realism many of us face as we travel the road before us.

You will find familiar characters introduced in Behind the Glass door as I attempt to sum up the events and deaths of Samantha Stone and Maddie Morgan. I do not format or outline the book. I simply let the universe offer me what it will, then I create what has been given to me.

It is my hope that you will enjoy.

TABLE OF CONTENTS

THE SOUL LIVES ON

We are fragile in the world of wonder and mystery as the magnificent universe continues to swirl around those of us who are alive and thriving. In death we are never truly gone but we are swept away by the musical rhythm of the audible sounds moving round this grand massive world, as it takes our souls on a new journey and into a new life. Know that the human spirit remains and is only a dimension away.

Always love those you hold dear and tell them of your feelings for never should you have to say, 'I'm sorry.'

The best of life happens when we take the opportunity to explore uncharted dreams, to reach for the unimaginable treasures your heart may hold. We must find the strength to wipe away all fears and take the chance of humiliation and failure, only to realize that it can be done, we can succeed.

Cherish the smallest things in life. Listen to the wind, enjoy a sunny day sing and dance as easy as water flows. And of all things listen to your voice as it whispers on the wind swishing by ever so quickly. Those words speak truth from your soul and are meant for you to realize.

Chapter 1
FIFTEEN YEARS LATER

From a perch high on the cliffs in Martha's Vineyard the winds were whipping loudly in the brilliance of a clear sunny day. Newly engaged Johnny Stone and Haley Morgan embraced one another as they leaned against an old weather-beaten wooden railing, surrounding the grounds of their newly purchased cottage style home. Together they listened to the cawing of the gulls and slapping of high sea grass as they stared at the vastness of the Atlantic Ocean watching swollen waves crash against the jagged coastline below. A million thoughts passed through their minds as they stood in silence embracing the past that brought them together and the future that awaited them as a married couple.

The years had flown by, and the loss of Samantha Stone and Maddie Morgan never faded from the minds of either of their children. Both Johnny and Haley had graduated college, earned their master's degrees, and worked in their perspective fields for ten years before reuniting quite by accident, at a conference in Chicago.

A sea of FBI agents mingled together amongst lots of chatter and the clinking of dishes, and boisterous laughter. This lecture was exciting as it was addressing old Cold Case files and the newest forensic data.

Johnny and Haley sat in different areas of the conference room yet often stretched their necks to capture a view of the other in the dimly lit room. At the end of the lecture, they both made a conscientious attempt to meet in the lobby area. At first there was a familiarity as they searched each other's faces trying to find the missing link, between them. A badge that bore their names finally put all suspicions to rest and they shyly embraced one another remembering their teenage crush. As their eyes met on that fateful day, the sparks reignited once again, as they had when they were teenagers, the rest would soon be history.

"Time and circumstances had taken Haley and me in different directions through the years. After writing back and forth in our first year in college, we lost touch. We were now in our early thirties and met quite by chance right here at the Hyatt Regency on Wacker Drive, in Chicago. Haley had grown into a beautiful woman, her brownish hair had subtle streaks of blonde highlights that framed her delicate face, which exaggerated her violet blue eyes. Upon our meeting Haley tentatively handed me her card when I asked for it; in turn, I slipped my card into her pocket promising to give her a call when I returned from a case I was working on in California."

Haley could not help but notice how handsome and strapping John had become. He stood six feet four inches tall with a strawberry blonde color to his hair, which was much like his mother had. He wore dimples in both of his cheeks and walked with the gate of a cougar and that certainly intrigued Haley. There was no doubt that Haley was nervous and butterflies took over her stomach at first glance of Johnny. It was not long after that the two of them were spending all their time together. Weeks turned into months and the two found themselves inseparable and undoubtedly falling in love.

Unbeknownst to Johnny, Haley was working a missing person and probable murder case, which had similarities to her mother's car accident and was a nightmare that continued to haunt her throughout the years. That case inspired her to investigate her own mom's death.

It was the evening of March 15th when Haley arrived at her New York apartment. She found the door ajar and thought perhaps it was Johnny with a surprise visit. As she pushed the door open calling out his name, she was met with silence then a thud, footsteps, and the slam of her back door. Immediately, she went for her gun which she kept in a nearby drawer, yet it was missing. She noticed that papers were scattered on the floor, and someone had rummaged throughout the entire place. Frightened, she went for the twenty-two she kept in her purse and did a swept through the apartment before she called her partner to report her issued revolver missing. Several agents arrived and took what information Haley could provide then searched for fingerprints or any DNA left behind by the perpetrator.

Haley had suspicions that she was being watched and followed but tried to tell herself that she was being paranoid and dramatic. Since she had been seeing Johnny, she noticed that her new neighbor was always peering out her window scanning her apartment. On occasion the woman would wave to Haley from her place across the street, which unsettle her further. Haley noticed that her neighbor appeared to be an older woman with long gray hair and figured her to be a nosy, lonely old gal. Haley let it go believing her to be harmless.

The agents advised Haley to go stay with her best friend Jan another agent, until they could figure out what had gone on in the apartment. As the agents waited outside Haley moved into her bedroom and bent down, unzipped the mattress cover, and pulled paperwork from it and evidence she had been gathering on Sam Stone and her mother, Maddie Morgan's cold case files. In her valise she packed clothing and toiletries to last for several days, until it was safe for her to return home.

After days of investigation, it was determined that the culprit could have been renegade thugs from the neighborhood looking for weapons or drugs, but who knew for sure? It was evident that Haley would have to move into a new place until her work on the Johnson's missing person case was resolved. Meanwhile, she would be with Jan until the department could relocate her.

Johnny was livid to learn that Haley had not shared the home invasion incident with him, she made light of it, not wanting him to worry. They decided it would be best to move out to the Vineyard as soon as possible to get away from the city and start their wedding plans.

⟲⟳ PATRICK'S VOICE ⟲⟳

"After arriving on the island, we reminisced, realizing time had quickly flown by and agreed that the road to recovery was long and painful regarding the loss of our mother's. After all this time, I would still have stabbing chest pain at the thought of my mother's death and my father's possible involvement in her demise. The very thought that my father could be involved provoked me to change my first name from Johnny his namesake, to Patrick, my middle name.

My father's abrupt disappearance upon my mother's passing, leaving me and my sister Julieann parentless as we began our first year at Villanova. I wanted nothing to do with him nor, to be reminded of him in any way. To this day I cannot fathom why he would do such an unconscionable thing to either of us.

He simply vanished into thin air. Back then, there were suspicions that he left the country to live on a tropical island with one of his many lovers. Whatever investigations were done at that time certainly brought nothing to the table. Yet, times have changed and so have forensics and the way people are tracked these days. In time, I promised myself that I would open this cold case file and find the truth to what had taken my mother's life.

Haley and I had become engaged within two years of dating and looked forward to our new life on Martha's Vineyard; a place we both loved. Our courtship was brief, yet intense as we both had a desire to have family and a sense of belonging to something and someone special. When our mothers died so closely to one another our worlds fell apart leaving a cold distant feeling to life itself. We agreed that our mourning needed to have new life. Our union in marriage and the love we felt for one another would allow a new breath of freedom for both of us.

The binding of our lives would be quite different from our Christmas Holiday visit on Newcomb Drive in Mallory Cove during the most tumultuous years in my sister Julieann's and my life.

In that time of our senior year of high school my parents were in the process of divorce. My mother was offered a job opportunity in Wisconsin where she could use her skills as an artist, drafter, and designer. At the same time, she would be living and working at Morgana Design Center with Maddie and Devin Morgan. They had been her best friends from Westport, who had moved out that way for a new beginning from their days in their Southern Connecticut old neighborhood.

Yes, I was now an FBI agent seeking Justice for those who could no longer speak for themselves. Haley worked as an FBI researcher. She had lost her mother in a suspicious car accident, prior to my mother's death. All questions pertaining to their cases were left unanswered, and no perpetrator was found in either case. This left us haunted. Together, we supported one another and looked to the future and a resolve to the mysteries left for us to unravel.

Through the years I had stayed connected with Detective Diane George and Lieutenant Kevin Dillon, who promised to keep their cold case files and our mothers' memories alive. The very thought that now I could assist the Mallory Cove investigative team was thrilling, giving me the resolve to push forward and end these enigmas frozen in time.

In preparation of our life together, Haley and I purchased our four-bedroom enchanted cottage style home in a hilly neighborhood on the bluffs in Chilmark on Martha's Vineyard. For the first five months we could only use the house on scattered weekends as we had to complete assignments in New York city. We believed ourselves to be blessed, owning a home that sat at the bottom of a bluff, where we shared incredible ocean views with the neighbors that towered above us.

Some, of our friends offered to help us move to the Island and we took advantage of their kind assistance as we partied in the afternoons after our work was completed. I rented a sailboat from the marina, and we enjoyed sunset weekend sails. It was our thanks to each of them for helping us.

Haley and I each had personal treasures, which followed us everywhere we went. They were simple personal effects belonging to our mom's, memories of these two beautiful women that we could never let go of nor let anyone else touch or move. It was well understood by our friends and they respected our request to leave certain boxes alone.

As we began to settle in, Haley often had the feeling that our house was being watched. She would often mention how uncomfortable she felt. I let it go until one night when I heard a scream coming from her office on the second floor. I ran into the room to find Haley panicked bent over hyperventilating.

"What, what is wrong?" I asked. She wept and had a look of panic glued to her face. I held her in my arms telling her that everything was all right as I continued my line of questioning, but Haley remained uncontrollable, tremoring, and carrying on hysterically. I grabbed her shoulders and gave her a shake, hoping she would snap out of it."

"What is it?" I asked with trepidation.

"Shut off the lights." She demanded.

"Now look out the window to the house above us. Someone is watching me with a telescope. Do you see him?"

"Honey, I don't see anything. Your imagination is playing tricks on you. They are probably looking at the stars and beyond to the ocean. It will take time for us to get use to our new surroundings and until we meet our neighbors you need to get a hold of yourself."

"Patrick, I'm not crazy, nor am I being too sensitive. I know what I feel and see. Please, do not doubt or insult my sense of knowing. I have an ominous feeling about this place and our neighbors."

"Over the weekend we'll head up the hill and introduce ourselves to whomever they are. Perhaps that will settle your nerves."

The very next morning we took a walk around the neighborhood, introducing ourselves to several folks in the circle of homes near us. Many neighbors were friendly and had small tales to tell. The last introduction we made was with Dr. Ferron Michaels, who worked for the Woods Hole Institute of Oceanography and his lovely wife Olivia, a nurse who worked for a home health agency in town. They too, had moved to the island from New York City to enjoy a peaceful life, surrounded by the beauty of nature. Our new acquaintance with the Michaels clicked, and we made plans to get together soon. We thanked them for their kindness and made our way up the hill to the mystery house.

I banged on the door as Haley stood shaking at the prospect of who might answer. I banged again then rang the bell and even hollered out hoping someone would hear me. But nothing! We were disappointed and withdrew back to our own home, where we tended to the exterior of our house and the gardens that needed our attention and nurturing prior to our wedding day.

"As the weeks went by, we spent much of our time working diligently on the outside lawn and landscape. We were less than a month away and certainly excited for our special day to arrive.

We chose to have our ceremony at a quaint old church, built in the late 1800s. Our reception was to be held in the back yard of our home for our best friends and what little family we had left. The ocean views and natural roses that adorned our yard would be the perfect scene for our reception. Haley was happy with the simplicity of the setting, and I was relieved that we could be outside enjoying nature instead of partying in a stuffy reception hall.

Haley was ecstatic about our upcoming nuptials. However, she still complained that she was being spied upon by those who lived above us. Unbeknownst to her, I had taken a swing by the mystery house on several occasions to introduce myself. Much to my disappointment there was never an answer to my knocking even though I could hear music coming from inside. Now, I was beginning to feel uncomfortable as well, but thought they were weekend dwellers, or that the owners rented the place out. I would play the waiting game and watch for movement on the property. In the meanwhile, I went to townhall to find out who owned the stately place, thinking that would easily remedy our inquisition."

Townhall never seemed to be open when I visited, so I began to ask questions on the computer. I was given limited times when someone would be in the office to assist me. My job took me off Island frequently and I had no time to chase down their personnel. It seemed, that the property above us, was purchased one month after we had bought our home, while we were still living in the city. An older couple by the name of Steven and Sharon Samuels from New York bought the place for a staggering price.

Haley inherited her father Devin's green thumb and took to gardening out back preparing for his visit in the weeks to come. Devin planned to stay for several months. He would arrive four days before the wedding and stay on while we honeymooned. We were delighted to have him. I was well aware of how much Haley missed her dad, needing him more than ever at this momentous time in her life.

Sadly, Haley's dad never remarried after her mom's car accident in Malloy Cove years ago. He enjoyed his friends, golfing and traveling. His dream business at Morgana Design was up for sale, and he looked forward to finding a small place here on the island for his retirement. He mentioned to us that he had invited a friend of his to be his partner at the wedding, with our permission, of course. Certainly, he did not need permission for anything, yet his thoughtfulness, was appreciated.

This was the first we heard of a woman in his life, and we were excited to know that finally he trusted enough to share time with someone special.

"Who is it, Dad? Can you share?"

"Nope, I want it to be a surprise."

Patrick and I let the topic go, knowing whoever she was, she would be here soon enough.

Chapter 2
MEETING THE NEIGHBORS

Patrick and I both showered after a long day of planting and installing some picket white fencing. As soon as we nestled onto the couch with our Tequila Sun-rises, the doorbell rang unexpectedly. Very much to our surprise there stood a tall very handsome Ferron Michaels and his stunning wife Olivia, each carried an abundance of food. Baked chicken, shrimp, green salad, and a pan of garlic brussel sprouts sprinkled with Italian cheese. We welcomed our new guests inside. Patrick made drinks and I retrieved cheese, crackers, and fruit to add to our impromptu dinner.

After gorging ourselves there was lots, of chit chat between us. Patrick took Ferron outside to show him the progress we had made in the garden area. Olivia and I stayed inside cleaning up. I could not help but wonder if Olivia had a job to keep herself busy. She confessed that she worked part time for the Samuel's on the hill above us.

"Really?" I asked with a surprised twist in my voice. "Are they nice people? I often get the feeling they are watching us very closely and quite honestly it leaves me unsettled. We have gone up the hill often to meet them, but they never answer the door. What's that all about?"

"I work for them a few days a week taking care of Mr. Samuels who is a very odd man, if you ask me. He had broken his leg quite badly in a fall months ago and spends much of his time in a wheelchair. Often, when he is oblivious to my whereabouts in the house, I find him walking around doing odd jobs as if there was nothing at all wrong with him. He has no limp or other infirmities. He seems to bend and move with ease. He insists on my giving him bed baths as he tells me of his past endeavors. The way he looks at me is flirtatious giving me a very uneasy feeling. You would think that his odd wife would take care of any of his personal needs leaving that out of my job description."

"His wife Sharon used to be incredibly beautiful in her younger days. She wore her hair long, flowing down her back. A full-length photo of her exposed her perfect figure. Other pictures of her adorned end tables and walls within the house. Those photos were the only visible artwork that adorned the walls and tabletops; leaving me to think that she might be a narcissist.

My position there is not much of a caretaker but more like a house-keeper, doing laundry and making beds. I get the idea that they just want the company and someone to talk to. They have asked me about you and Patrick and seem to take quite an interest in the both of you, asking if I know anything about your families. I thought that to be presumptuous. As you know, I know nothing of you, so I certainly couldn't answer many of their questions."

"Really, I wonder what's up with that? What kind of questions were they asking you Olivia?"

"They asked me where you were from, where you went to school and wanted to know about your parents on both sides. Mr. Samuels especially had an interest in Samantha Stone and the mystery surrounding Maddie Morgan's car accident."

"Now, how would he know anything about that? And why would he be interested in Patrick's mother or even mine for that matter? That seems a bit sick to me."

"I'm not sure Haley. They are awkward busy bodies. They did a search about you on the computer. Many people like to know who their neighbors are, especially in these times of change and so much distrust."

"Olivia, do you happen to know if they have a telescope on their third floor? I often have seen someone looking directly into our second-floor windows. And that, gives me the heebie-jeebies. Could you do some investigating for me?"

"Sure, I'm going there on Friday so I'll see what I can find out for you."

"Whatever you do Olivia, don't tell them I was asking about them. I don't want to start a problem with my new neighbors. You know?"

"Not to worry Haley, I've got you covered."

Ferron and Patrick arrived back inside as if on que. We had one more round of drinks and bid our farewell for the evening. At least I have someone on the inside that can find out about my suspicions. I did not say a word to Patrick for fear of what he would think or do. The ball was now in motion, and I felt a sense of relief as Patrick was on the mainland working on a case that took him away for most of the week - leaving me to feel insecure and vulnerable.

I had not seen Oliva for the next few days and wondered if she had been able to find out about the mystery telescope or anything else going on at the house on the hill.

An abrupt knock on the door startled me. I answered it and was shocked to see an older lady with long stringy gray- hair and poorly cared for teeth, beaming a smile at me. My immediate thought was of the wicked witch from a certain fairy tale, minus her broom, of course.

"Hello, may I help you?" I asked.

"My name is Sharon Samuels. I live on the hill above you. I'm sorry I didn't get down here sooner to introduce myself, but by husband is not well. Here, this is for you."

She stretched her hands out to offer a platter of cookies for Patrick and me.

Suddenly, I felt a surge of guilt as my face turned red. My body tingled with fear as sweat beaded up on my forehead. Did she know that I was meddling in her business? Did she know that Olivia was investigating them, on my behalf?

I stuck one hand out to take the cookies from her and with the other hand I shook hers and found a cold wet clammy, limp shake of greeting. I was a bit horrified and embarrassed. Quickly, I told her how sorry I was to hear that her husband was not feeling well, which broke the awkwardness of our meeting.

"I hope he gets well soon."

I gave her a quick smile and thanked her for her kind gesture. Immediately, I calculated that she was lying after what Olivia had told me of Mr. Samuels' agility.

Boldly, she asked if she could come in and took a step forward as if to push herself into the house. Nervously, I told her I was on my way out to run errands and suggested that another time would be better. A look of disappointment crossed her face as I closed the door with my heart pounding, ending our brief encounter, which left me fearful.

I grabbed my purse and keys making sure to lock the house up tight. At the end of the driveway, I saw Olivia making her way up to my car. I unlocked the door and told her to get in, she did without hesitation. I quickly explained to her of my brief encounter with Sharon telling her of the cookies she had made for Patrick and me. She was shocked, as she explained that Sharon does not cook or bake but thought her offering was kind. I, on the other hand, was suspicious and promised myself to pitch them into the garbage as soon as I returned home.

"Where are we going?" Olivia asked. I told her that I was on my way to the florist to make last minute changes to the list of floral arrangements for the wedding. We both gave a nod and a wave to Sharon as she made her way back up to her hillside home.

Olivia and I were gone for two hours stopping by antique shops along the way. We found an old anchor which I thought would look great on the side of the shed, which was a backdrop for one of my favorite gardens. It was a perfect touch for my house by the sea.

We arrived back home in time to see Sharon leaving the back gated area that protected my gardens.

I stopped the car and shouted to Sharon asking her what she was doing.

"Oh, just enjoying all your challenging work, it looks great. Hi Olivia, I see you have made a new friend. Have a good day; I need to get back to Steven."

I hollered out to Sharon asking her with a pitched voice, not to enter the backyard as we were preparing it for our wedding in a few weeks. I could not help but wonder if she had been there the whole time that we were gone. Olivia and I looked at each other perplexed, figuring she might be a bit senile. We did not think much of it until we entered the house and found everything in disarray.

"I can't believe she entered the house without anyone being home. Boy, that was pretty ballsey."

The hair on the back of my neck stood straight up, even Olivia was shocked to find the kitchen a mess as if the old girl from up the hill helped herself to food and drink. I felt it necessary to call Patrick and let him know what was going on. Both he and Olivia insisted that I call the police.

I did put out a call and while we waited Olivia and I made a drink and wandered out to the back yard to sit and wait, keeping a close eye on the house above us.

"Oh, my God! Look over there to the back garden. Who would do such a thing?"

The whole garden was a mess, dirt overturned, and the flowers had been dug up, and thrown over the fence. A scruffy old dog leash was hanging over the fence having somehow gotten caught on one of the fence picks.

"Why would she do such a thing? We'll have the police ask the questions as I don't want to go head-to-head with her especially if she has mental illness."

Olivia just shook her head and gave me a look of shock or was it more like guilt? She was hard to read. Then she said. "It could have been her dog, that scruffy little thing is a nuisance at their house as well. I'm so sorry Haley."

"Well, it's back to the nursery. Now I have to replace all that's been lost here."

Just then a cruiser pulled up into the driveway. The vehicle was an older model SUV with dents and discoloration of its body paint. Red and white lights flashed furiously from their crooked perch on the roof of the vehicle. Olivia and I met the officer outside and invited him in so as not to be watched by my neighbors on the hill. We explained what happened as best we were able, yet, since we did not see it happen, we could only assume.

"Ma'am, I'll have a chat with your neighbor's right now. Not to worry. I'll be back shortly to let you know the results of our conversation."

Hours later there was nothing and no return of the officer. I thought perhaps that he did not think it was important enough to follow up with me. Olivia waited for as long as she could, then headed home to do chores at her house. She suggested that the Constable may have had another more important call to answer. I agreed, figuring she might be right.

I took pictures of the mess in the kitchen and garden areas and showed them to the Constable but found it very suspicious that he did not dust for prints or take any photo evidence with him. Of course, he did say he would get back to me with any information. After thinking twice about how I would have investigated the scene, I decided I was used to how the FBI did things and this was vastly different from their procedures.

Another day passed and still no news from the police or the investigating constable yet, I found comfort in knowing that Patrick and Ferron would both return on Friday evening.

I was lonely and feeling nervous about good old Sharon and her weird behavior. I put out a call to Olivia and asked if she would join me for dinner. She gladly accepted my invitation. That evening Olivia and I made dinner and drinks. In the background the television came out with a blaring alert that one of their Constables was missing and had not been heard from for over 48 hours. A photo of a cubby faced gray-haired man appeared on screen. His name was James Harrison. He was the very same constable that had been at my house two days before.

An abrupt knock on the door quickly brought me to my feet. My new friend stood next to me as I swung the door open to find men in uniform staring down at us. I told them of Sharon Samuels' visit and of her odd behavior. Olivia interjected, as she filled them in on her position as healthcare worker at the Samuels' residence. Once satisfied the officers left finding their way up the hill to further investigate.

Olivia and I turned towards each other and in an instant decided to become detectives ourselves. We headed to the second floor to watch for any intervention at the neighbor's house. The officers searched the driveway for tire tracks. Casts were lifted from the sandy area where constable Harrison had parked his vehicle. The officers banged on the door loud enough that we could hear them all the way down the hill, yet again, no one answered. I figured the Samuels had to be home as the lights were on, even in the attic.

As the days passed, we noticed that their house was under constant surveillance as unmarked vehicles were now predominant fixtures in the neighborhood. But where could the Samuels be? And why weren't they answering the police who were banging loudly at their door? Olivia was due to be at the Samuels' house the next day. I cautioned her to be vigilant and I certainly hoped she would have some kind of answers for me.

Chapter 3
DAY OF RECKONING

I awoke Friday morning with anxiety and a pain in the pit of my stomach. I knew that Olivia would be working at the house on the hill and worried for her safety yet, I waited with great anticipation for any information she might provide.

I made myself busy by working in the gardens as I kept a close eye on the house above ours. Olivia made her way up the hill and knocked on the door, no answer. She then rang and clanged the dinner bell that hung on the porch. Finally, the door opened, and Olivia disappeared inside. My heart pounded with excitement and fear.

I filled my time constructively by turning my attention to the garden and began replacing all the flowers that had been destroyed. Suddenly, my cell phone began its melodic song, I knew Patrick was on the other end.

"Good morning honey. When will you be home? I'm anxious for you to get here."

"I'm on the ferry now and should be there within an hour or so. I miss you and know you must be out of your mind with worry."

"Oh, thank God you're not too far out, Patrick. You certainly do know me well. Olivia is working for the Samuels today and I am concerned about her. Did you see the news about the missing Constable out here? Patrick, he was the same man who came to the house when I called about Sharon's visit and the destruction she did here. The constable went up the hill to their home to investigate, telling me he would be back with a report. But he never came back, nor did he call. Olivia and I surmised that he had gotten a more urgent case and would get back to me in a day or two with results."

"Haley, I'll be there soon, and we'll go over everything. I was working a case and could not call you; I am sorry. Forgive me?"

"See you soon, I love you."

"Love you too."

By noon Patrick's vehicle roared down from over the hill pulling left into the driveway. I was elated that he was home and met him with a run into his arms. I was a floodgate of emotions, tears overflowed as if a damn had burst, reliving my week of anxiety.

"It's all right Haley, I'm here now and have taken time off through our honeymoon. This way I can help to settle us both in, as we await your dad. He is due next Tuesday. Not only that, but I am not comfortable leaving you alone these days. We'll figure everything out."

"Thank you, Patrick, I appreciate your sensitivity."

We sat for a time as I filled him in on all the odd things that took place during his absence. I also showed him the pictures of Sharon's intrusive visit. Then told him of her gift of cookies that I pitched into the garbage. He was shocked that she would be so bold and told me that he would make a visit up the hill in the afternoon. Then he demanded me to stay away from both of the Samuels. A sudden alarm from my phone told me that Olivia had left a message. It simply said.

"Yes, telescope on third floor facing in your direction. Chat later."

"You see Patrick, I was right. Olivia just texted me that there is a telescope on the third floor of the Samuels' home, and it is facing towards the back of our house."

"Haley, leave this to the police. Do not try to figure this out yourselves. Do you hear me?"

Only a slight rise of my lips alluded to a smile, of sorts. Patrick knew me well and realized that I would not let go until I had the answers I needed. They were a very weird couple from what I could tell. Hours later the phone rang franticly. I answered to find Olivia's voice quivering on the other end.

"I have to stop by after dark tonight as I can't take the chance of letting the Samuels see me at your house. Make sure to shut your outside lights off."

"That's fine. Bring Ferron along, we'll make a late dinner."

"Ok, will do." Click.

The sun had set by 8:30 and our company arrived soon after. Olivia grabbed my hand pulling me toward the couch.

"Sit down, she demanded."

"Olivia, what happened to your face? You have a shiner there and cuts on your cheeks and lips."

"That is Mr. Samuels' handy work. I wandered away from both he and his wife, making my way to the attic. Soon, I heard the door open and the creaking of footsteps on the staircase. I looked over and Steven was standing behind me asking in a raged voice why I had come to the third floor. I scrambled for words telling him I didn't know if anything needed to be cleaned on that level. His eyes changed to black, his voice in a loud gravely tone told me to keep my nose out of his business.

He then grabbed an old plastic baseball bat hanging on the wall, one that must have been left by the previous owners. As I looked over at him, I was hit in the head with the swing of bat that caught me exactly right it was followed by a hard punch to my face. My heart raced not knowing if he would back off or continue battering me further.

Of course, the Mrs. had joined us on the third floor apologizing profusely, saying they were sorry and did not mean any harm. Sharon became excited telling me it was an accident, and that Steven would sometimes act out his frustrations as she continued her sweet apologies. Steven glared at Sharon as if she might be next on his list of abuses."

"I brushed by Steven giving him a look that could kill as Sharon followed close behind. I made my way to the kitchen where she insisted on putting cold packs on my eyes and lips. I refused wanting to leave but she came upon me quickly with a wet cloth to wipe the blood from my face. I sat in a kitchen chair where I gazed at the floor under the table. There were blood stains just as clear as day and a line of smeared blood leading to the back door. Immediately, I thought of Constable Harrison and wondered if he met with ill fate, right where I sat."

"My mind was spinning with a million questions as I made up scenarios to explain what I had seen. After a few moments, I insisted that I was fine and needed to get home as Ferron would be arriving soon. I refused to let Sharon get another word in edgewise and scrambled toward the front door.

Steven stood silently holding onto the doorknob wearing a Cheshire cat like grin from ear to ear. He looked like a lunatic from an insane asylum. Those people have serious issues, there is no doubting that. I'll tell you Haley, I never moved so fast in all my life. With my bags in hand, I fled out of the house leaving Steven to gawk at me with a menacing glare."

"We'll see you next Tuesday," he whispered.

"I simply nodded my head, as a chill ran my blood cold."

Patrick and Ferron were both absolutely infuriated with Steven and decided to take a walk up the hill to visit the Samuels regardless of the hour. They found the front door open as if to welcome them. Each called out.

"Hello is anyone here? Is anyone here?"

An echo rang back at them as the massive room had little furniture in it to absorb the sound. Footsteps soon came from down the hall and there stood Sharon in a revealing nightgown. Both Patrick and Ferron turn their heads in embarrassment as Sharon asked what they wanted.

"Sorry Ma'am but your front door was unlocked and the door was open."

Ferron stumbled awkwardly into conversation asking what had happened to his wife's eye and the cuts on her face and lips. Sharon explained that her husband was touched, as she called it, and sometimes would act inappropriately. She professed her apologies saying it was late, hinting at the fact that she wanted them both gone.

Patrick then interrupted asking why she had gone to his home and trashed the garden and broke into the house helping herself to whatever she wanted. Sharon looked shocked and said it was not she who had done such a thing. She then walked toward the opened door nearly pushing them outside. It was evident that they both suffered from dementia and not of their right minds. Or were they?

"Don't you ever lay a hand on my wife again or I'll have you arrested. Do you understand?" Ferron asked with fury in his voice.

Patrick also piped up stating that they were not welcome on his property unless they came by way of the front door and do not under any circumstances enter our backyard. "Understood?" Expressionless, Sharon simply smiled as her eyes squinted and turned a shade of gray.

The two men walked back down the hill shaking their heads in disbelief.

"Great! Our new neighbors are whackos. I'll call the police in the morning to report all of this and see if anyone has news of Constable Harrison."

The next morning Patrick called the police. Soon, an officer arrived at the house to gather information on the Samuels once again. Ferron and Olivia were in attendance as she wanted them to see first-hand her face and the damage done by Steven. Olivia also told them she saw blood stains and apparent blood smears across the kitchen floor of the Samuels' house. That raised the brow of the investigator who was still awaiting his search warrant for their house.

The police stated that these were real crimes, and their intent was to arrest the Samuels for assault and battery, breaking and entering with property damage as well as criminal mischief. The families agreed that something should be done to set the ground rules for the new neighbors.

Not long after the police left Patrick's house, they saw the Samuels being led to the cruiser to be taken to the Police department for questioning.

Chapter 4
WEDDING PLANS

Ferron and Olivia joined us for the final garden touches in preparation for the wedding. Gifts began to arrive and were placed in a corner of the living room, each had decorative bows and cards with well wishes.

Last-minute details for the florist and caterer were sent over the computer for the final overview.

We decided to have a tent canopy over the guests and band in the event of rain and were excited that everything was coming together nicely. Our nerves were now relaxed with the last-minute changes and I for one was satisfied with Patrick's intervention with the Samuels.

By three pm a ring of the doorbell sent Olivia to answer the call. A very tall detective stood towering over her.

"Haley, you have a guest, it's the police."

Patrick and Ferron joined their wives in the living room as a six-foot-tall constable towered over them.

"Yes sir, how can we help you?" Patrick asked.

"Well, sir it seems that your neighbors, do suffer from dementia or they're damn good actors. However, we took fingerprints from both and have found that Mr. Samuels has no fingerprints to offer as the tips on all his fingers have been burnt off, only leaving scars on his fingers and the palms of his hands. He stated that it was from a car fire years ago when he worked on engines. We are continuing our investigation into their backgrounds, but this will take some time. However, we believe their names could be aliases as we have no record of Steven or Sharon Samuels of their age. We did find a young couple in their thirties by those names who are now deceased due to a car accident about five years ago. Please be patient!

"Did you look into the blood I saw on the kitchen floor?" Olivia inquired.

"Yes, we know what you have told us in that regard, and we have spoken to the Judge about securing a search warrant as we speak. When we receive it, we will go over the house with a fine-tooth comb. Our forensic teams should be in their house later this afternoon or first thing in the morning, I can't give you any further information at this time."

"Thank you for sharing with us what you could. And if you need my help, I am with the FBI." Patrick said.

"Thank you, sir. If we have a need, we will call upon you. Good day." They all sat stunned for a moment before returning to the tasks at hand. Devin would be arriving the next day. His bed still needed to be made as well as the room for his date. I stopped for a moment wondering if they preferred to sleep in the same bed. Suddenly, I felt like a parent setting up rules for the adults to follow in my new home, this certainly was a role reversal. How silly of me, came to mind. I will let them decide where they want to sleep when they arrive.

Olivia could tell I had a thousand things on my mind. She and Ferron decided to call it a night bidding their farewells. From the darkness Olivia whispered over her shoulder, "See you tomorrow."

"See you then." I returned her salutation with a whisper as well.

⟲ DAD'S ARRIVAL ⟳

My sleep was restless through the night knowing my father would be arriving in the morning. It had been at least eight months since I had seen him, and I swelled with ecstatic anticipation awaiting his arrival.

UPS and Amazon trucks began arriving early in the morning bringing more gifts for the wedding. We were grateful for the kindness our family and friends were bestowing upon us. We grabbed a cup of coffee and some breakfast rolls then headed out back to sit by the garden and view the ocean, enjoying the smells of sweet tea roses and thick salty sea air. We truly were living our dreams.

Silently, a black limousine came from the hill above and stopped right in front of the house. Pat and I came around from the outside patio in time to greet my father as he stepped out of the limo. I threw myself into his arms and was swung around in a circle just like he did when I was a little girl. Happiness gushed from both of us. He then turned from me and reached his hand into the limo to retrieve his date. A slender arm shone in the sunlight then a long pale leg slid its way to the ground. Patrick and I were dumbfounded as the woman raised her head to greet us, a sudden burst of laughter and joy came from Patrick as he put his arms around the woman hugging her tightly and shedding a tear.

"Haley, I don't know if you remember Liv Johnson? She was an incredibly good friend of Julieann's and mine from the Westport neighborhood and she was also the nurse that took care of my mother in the hospital."

Haley was confused a bit and spun around giving her father a questioning look. Haley you were away at school at the time your mother's death and Sam's passing, so, I don't think you would remember Liv. Let's go inside and I'll explain everything to you." Devin said.

After a brief tour of the house and gardens the foursome took to the living room with coffee in hand.

"So, Dad, please tell me about Liv." Devin smiled as he lowered his head and I gave Liv an accepting expression, calming any fears she may have had.

"I met Liv quite by chance in a phone conversation some years ago when Sam was a patient of hers. She had called to ask me if I knew anything about her medical condition. At that time, Sam was not doing well and there was concern that there might have been foul play regarding her illness. Sadly, I had nothing to offer her. Liv was truly kind and promised to keep me informed of her progress and she did.

After Sam's death we had the opportunity to meet at a remembrance gathering given by Sam's side of the family out on the Cape. Liv and I kept an ongoing long-distance phone relationship alive through the years. Finally, I decided I was being ridiculous not to spend personal time with Liv getting to know her more intimately and learn all the facets in her life. I invited her out to Mallory Cove for vacation and we hit it off nicely. There is an extreme age difference between us, one that we are not at all concerned about. Some, however, do give us the highbrow thinking I am her father. Liv's youth and exuberance for life was exactly what I needed to awaken me to the fact that not every woman is like Maddie, no disrespect intended, Haley. One day, I will share with you what my relationship with your mother was all about. Liv and I are incredibly happy and live each day as though it were our last."

"Dad as long as you are both happy that's good enough for me. I'm just elated that you have returned to life, it's nice to have you back."

"Let me show you to your rooms." Patrick piped up. We took them to the second floor allowing them to choose where they wanted to stay. They easily chose the master suite with the private bath, which, seemed to settle any questions I had about whether they would stay as singles or as a couple.

"I imagine you must be hungry, let's head downstairs. We've prepared a spread for you."

"I'm not sure about Devin but I'm ravenous." Liv said as she rubbed her belly.

I felt odd to know Dad was with another woman, but I would have to get used to it and stop thinking like a child and more like a mature adult. He had been alone for a long time and fate seems to have found its way to him. Liv is a genuinely nice woman with no ulterior motives or so it seems; and she certainly gives my dad looks that are loving and very sweet.

My Dad is worth a fortune with his businesses, properties, and the insurance policy he had on my mother. It left him set for several lifetimes. It always concerned me that some cougar would seek him out to secure for herself a safe, lucrative, and exciting life regardless of any true feelings for him. He deserved more than that and he found his true match in Liv Johnson, yet I couldn't help but wonder what dad wanted to share with me regarding his and mom's relationship.

Dad helped Patrick prepare breakfast while Liv and I took the trays out to the patio. Surprisingly, the doorbell rang with an urgency to it. My dad thought it was UPS delivering more gifts so, he decided to answer the call. He swung the door wide open to find a handsome black couple standing on our doorstep.

"Hi, you must be Devin, the couple blurted out."

"Yes, yes, I am. Let me call my daughter. Haley, you have guests here!" Devin turned to Haley with a questioning look on his face.

"Dad, I'd like you to meet our dear friends and neighbors. This is Dr. Ferron and Olivia Michaels."

Devin quickly extended his hand to greet them both, inviting them to come in and join us on the patio. Immediately, Devin dug right into a conversation wanting to know all about Ferron and where he was working as a physician. Ferron explained that he was a Doctor of Marine Biology at Woods Hole Oceanographic Institute. Devin beamed into life. He loved the sea and wanted to learn everything he could at his first meeting with Ferron. Realizing he was being rude, Devin turned to Olivia and apologized for not asking about her career before indulging himself in Ferron's exciting research at the Institute.

"I'm a nurse sir and most importantly a wife."

Small talk ensued as Liv and Devin were impressed with their daughter and son-in-law's new friends.

Olivia asked Haley if there was any news about the hill dwellers. Devin picked right up on her tone and asked what was wrong.

"Haley what is going on?" Devin's tone was one of concern.

"Oh, it's nothing dad except we have an odd couple up on the hill. Olivia, their caretaker, was assaulted by the old man when he found her in the attic of their house. She was doing me a favor looking for a telescope, as I often, feel as though someone is looking at me through the windows. I have seen them intruding on our privacy.

I reported this to the police, as well as the fact that the old woman had dug up our garden in the backyard and entered our house making a mess of everything. The officer went up to their home to speak with them and he has not been seen since."

"Be careful Haley you don't know how insane they might be or what they are capable of doing. What a frightening situation to be in." Devin said.

"We'll be fine dad; the police are on it and Patrick is doing some investigating of his own. I'm sure it will all work out just fine."

"You can never be too careful in this crazy world of ours."

"Yes, I am sure you are right but, I'm learning as I go."

"Look, before I forget, I have something for you and Patrick." Devin said.

Off he went to the second floor to retrieve his gifts. Devin had a sad look on his face as he asked Patrick and me to go into the sunporch of the house. He lowered his head and handed each of us a small, wrapped package.

It is time for the two of you to have these. I do not mean to bring on any kind of sadness but its time you learn the truth about what was going on at Newcomb Drive all those years ago. After much contemplation, I decided it was time to clear the house of your mom's belongings, Haley. In doing so I also found many of Sam's belongings including her diary. These diaries hold mysteries of their past and many of their life secrets. Within these pages you will find the answers you have been looking for. I'd like to suggest that you wait until after the honeymoon when you can relax, read, and take all this information in without upsetting the wedding."

"We can make you that promise Dad."

With skepticism Patrick smirked at me for having made such a promise. We decided to put their journals in the top dresser of our bureau where we knew they would be safe. The problem now was to shut off our minds for several weeks until we could concentrate on the mysteries held within each diary.

Chapter 5
THE DIARIES

B runch went on without a hitch. The Michaels,' my dad and Liv bonded as if they had known each other for years. Early afternoon gave way to a setting sun, and we gathered in the backyard overlooking the ocean and pure beauty nature offered. Within minutes the wind picked up sending sprays of sand all over us. We each turned in the direction of the house on the hill trying to avoid sand being blown in our eyes while feeling the powerful winds slap stinging sensations on our skin.

It was evident that the Samuels were home. All the lights were on sending a bright glow over the cliffs. Fear and anger gripped the Michaels, and I was visibly shaken.

"Let's go inside it's getting late and I'm sure Devin and Liv are exhausted; it has been a long day for them." Patrick said.

The Michael's took that as their que to head out. They said their goodnights with hugs and walked out into the approaching darkness. Dad and Liv retreated to their room on the second floor as Patrick and I cleaned up the kitchen before heading to bed, ourselves.

I was awakened during the night by the sounds of scratching on the back patio. A shadow slid across the window. I woke Patrick up with the news that there seemed to be a visitor in the backyard. Patrick grabbed his gun and carefully looked out the window to find that scruffy old dog belonging to the Samuels digging in the garden once again. Patrick went through the kitchen making enough noise to scare the dog off. There was a very tall man walking a dog off-leash in the early morning dawn. He was no one we had seen in the neighborhood before, but he must have been a guest of the Samuels, as he and that nuisance dog ascended the cliff disappearing into their driveway.

Once again, we would have to address our neighbors in the morning. This was beginning to get old, and I couldn't wait for the wedding to be over so I wouldn't have to worry about the yard and all the wedding fixtures that I did not want to replace again.

We all woke up at the crack of dawn. While having breakfast I asked dad and Liv if they had heard anything during the night.

"I thought I heard footsteps out back then a dog whining, but I'm not sure if it was only a dream or simply my own delirium." Liv said.

We laughed for a moment before going out back to enjoy the early morning. The garden had been disturbed again, but this time someone had taken the time to rake the area; leaving little for us to complain about. We had no choice but to watch the Samuels and their new guest.

Soon the rental company arrived to set up the tents, tables, chairs, and the serving stations we had ordered. Pat and I were so engrossed in directing where everything needed to go that we did not zero in on the tall gray-haired man taking Mr. Samuel's for his morning wheelchair ride until they had disappeared into the driveway leading to the Samuel's home. I figured; they had replaced Olivia with the gray-haired old man due to the abusive incident she had with the old geezer.

Many of our wedding guests arrived on the island and were staying at the B&B's that lined the cobblestone streets in town. As evening arrived, we joined the others for Patrick's Bachelor party, which included each of us.

We had a wonderful time, what we could remember of it. Dinner was fabulous and we were all a bit tipsy, to say the least. Two of Patrick's friends were our designated drivers making sure everyone arrived home safely. At 3 am we made our way down the hill to our house. Some of the guys were a bit rowdy and I had hoped they did not cause a stir with the neighbors, due to the late hour. We told everyone to stay at our house as we had plenty of room to accommodate our guests.

∞ MORNING SHOCKER ∞

Pat and I awoke early to the smell of booze permeating the entire house. Slowly, our guests crept into the kitchen with complaints of headaches and upset stomachs. On went the coffee and out came the antacids and Bloody-Mary's. We seemed to continue where the evening left off, less the hard liquor, of course. Suddenly, our focus was on the house, it seemed to have been ransacked. Someone was looking for something. Drawers had been pulled out and many of our gifts had been opened and discarded like junk. Was this Sharon indulging herself in our belongings again!?

We called the police complaining of another intrusion at our home. This time Patrick was infuriated and didn't wait to be accompanied by the cops. He and a few of the others headed up the hill for a confrontation, for the last time.

The doorbell rang several times before a tall gray-haired man answered the door. "May I help you sir? The man asked in a gravelly voice.

"Is Mr. Samuels home?" Patrick's voice was demanding.

"I'm sorry sir, he is indisposed at this time."

"Listen, this Mr. Samuels is never available to speak with me or anyone for that matter and we need a healthy conversation. You sir were seen in my yard, in the wee hours of this morning walking the Samuels' dog. Please tell me why you can't keep that damn dog out of my yard. We are getting ready for our wedding on Saturday, and we are sick and tired of cleaning up after that scruffy ole thing. It is not fair to me or my wife-to-be. If you cannot keep that dog away, we will come to Mr. Samuels for financial compensation. Give him my damn message!"

"I'm sorry sir, we'll be sure to keep him well out of your way. And congratulations to the both of you."

"Are you new here? We haven't seen you before."

"My name is Jonathan, I'm an old friend of the Samuels. They invited me for a short stay."

Patrick and the men left the porch and wondered why Jonathan's face was disfigured and covered with scars and burn marks, making him hard to look at. Those questions would have to wait, if ever they would be asked.

"Well, I think he got the point." Patrick said.

The men headed back to the house where the others were waiting. Brunch was served by 1:00 pm, then everyone left shortly thereafter to rest for the big day.

Haley and I went into the living room to clean up and stack the opened gifts trying to make sense of the mess someone had made. Voices were heard on the front porch, and we answered the door before the bell could be rung. Two officers asked about our call, and we immediately showed them into the living room so they could view the mess for themselves. This time they did take fingerprints and did get back to us within hours with the results.

It was apparent that Sharon Samuels was the culprit here, but there were no other prints found.

"I believe, she has dementia, Sir."

"Do you want to have her arrested for trespassing and several other offenses?"

"No just leave it be for now. I do not want my wife getting upset before the wedding we have too much on our plates right now. We will deal with her later."

After the police left, Haley ran into our room to check the drawers where she had placed the two gifts her father had given to us. Luckily, they were there, unharmed. She told Patrick that she feared something might happen to them and made the decision to break her promise to her dad and open her gift.

Inside her wrapped package she found a pale blue diary with gold writing on the cover that said, 'My Personal Diary.' On the first page in her mother's own handwriting, Haley found the words to be haunting. They read, 'Secrets to my screwed-up life.'

Immediately, Haley called to Patrick to see what she had received and pleaded with him to open his gift as well. Hesitantly, Patrick broke his promise too. There in his mother's favorite color pink was another diary simply entitled, 'My life, the trials and tribulations.'

Dad and Liv had gone into town leaving us the opportunity to delve into each of the dairies without their knowledge. Patrick took his little treasure into the sunroom, while I buried myself on the living room couch closely clutching my mothers' words and secrets.

For the next few hours, we searched the diaries for anything that might reveal the truth of what may have happened in their past lives and news that would bring light on each of their deaths.

Chapter 6
HALEY'S REVELATIONS

∞ DIARY SECRETS ROUND ONE ∞

The first few pages in my mother's diary were reminiscent of her youth and of what seemed to be promiscuous college days. This small book promised to be a tell all and I wasn't sure if I really wanted to know too much. However, I was eager to learn what I could about my mom. I had missed so much of her life, never having bonded as many mothers and daughters do. I thumbed through the beginning pages and learned how close she and Samantha had been; as explained, they were like glue. Sam was the strong one with ethics, religion, common sense, and good grades. While reading my mother's writing, I felt as though she may have had a streak of jealousy towards Sam calling her a goody two shoes and stiff. Sam always thought of God first and doing the right thing.

Her little diary also stated that my grandparents genuinely appreciated my mother's friendship with Sam as she was my mother's redeeming quality and a good example for her. She held up the family reputation externally.

A trip to New York sadly told of mom's abortion and how Sam and her boyfriend Joe took her into the city, then cared for her during her recovery. I was broken to know my own mother would have taken an innocent life. I tried to understand her actions reminding myself that she was a college student and faced being disowned by her parents.

After college, there was lots of promiscuity with hordes of men. My mother did have a sensitive side to her as she also wrote of happier times and falling in love with my dad. She told of their sailing days, yacht club parties and the many friends they had in those times.

She described their wedding day as a fairytale, fulfilling every dream she had ever imagined. My crazy mom was caught giving a lingering kiss to a guest my father didn't know but he let it go addressing it after the fact with a stern warning to my mom, reminding her that she was now a married woman. He was understanding and always made excuses for her. He simply thought her drunken state made sense for her thoughtless actions.

It was evident to me that my mother was a wild one, always taking chances in life and never thinking of the consequences that may follow. For a time, she and others used drugs, but my father refused to participate in any illegal activity.

My gloom turned into a ray of sunlight on the pages before me, reading that my dad was a good, decent man.

My mom explained that our move to Mallory Cove was due to my mother's need to get away from poisonous friends that were influential in the destructive decisions she made. She told how my father was nearly broken having to leave behind his brothers, sisters, and the business he worked so hard to establish in Westport. He sacrificed everything to save my mother and their marriage. It was obvious that he loved mom very much and took his wedding vows seriously.

Tears fell blurring the words on the page. My heart was broken with anguished disappointment as the fairytale story I always told myself about my mother, was nothing more than a lie. She was not at all the person I delusionally created her to be. Overwhelmed, I marked the page and slowly closed the diary wanting to digest what I had read.

Immediately, I wondered what it was that Patrick was learning about his own mother. I stood in the doorway of the sunroom and found Patrick reading with a smile on his face as tears fell into his lap.

"Are you alright?" I asked.

"Yes, just happy, that your dad saved these dairies for us to read. With that, Patrick looked up to see the devastated look on my face. "What's wrong Haley? You look like you've seen a ghost."

"I have. I answered. I just never knew my mother had a sinister side to her but it's all there in her own handwriting."

I began to share some of what I had learned about good ole Maddie and found Patrick apologizing for my mom's behavior.

"It's not your fault, Pat. I will get through the dairy and make a full assessment of the story she has told; I can tell you my father had his hands full with her. I feel so badly for him."

∞ SAMANTHA'S TELLING ∞

Patrick shared that his mother's story began in Westport and of the blessed life she lived with her incredible family. She told of the Christmas parties they had and the many people whom she did not know that attended each year. There was an indiscretion with Uncle Jack and a sales representative named Melissa. This woman had a horrible reputation for screwing any man who would have her. She frequented my father's office at the University, and it seems that my mother did not trust her. That one act of enthusiastic sexual activity in our pantry, during a Christmas party, destroyed Jack and Kara's marriage sending them to live in another part of the country.

"Um, I remember that incident vaguely, and often wondered why my parents' dear friends left the area."

My mother continued as she told of my father's talent and the fun they had singing as my dad played his famous piano concertos as they hosted the entire neighborhood for our Christmas parties. She went on to tell of their sailing days and how dad had bought mom, her very own 38-foot sailing vessel named 'Samantha's Rig'.

"We had so much fun in those days, fishing, diving off the sides of the boat, sun tanning on the decks and the many picnics we had as we sailed to deserted islands off the coast. Those were the best times of my life. I really miss that boat, and often wonder what my father did with her?"

Mom went on to tell of her psychiatrist Dr. Steven Silverman. She said my father had sent her there as he felt she was unstable and needed professional help. Somehow, she became sweet on the doctor, but nothing ever happened.

"I saw that doctor also when I was in high school. My mother wanted me to see him to help with my intuitive gifts, as she called them. I always had the feeling that he was a weirdo and always digging for more information about my mother. After a brief time, I stopped seeing him as he seemed distracted and not at all interested in me. Besides, college was on the horizon, and I had so much to do to get ready for the fall."

"Enough of all this for now. Your dad was right, we should save this information for after the wedding, when we can give these diaries our undivided attention. Agreed?"

"Yes, I agree. It's upsetting and who knows what else they will reveal?"

Haley could not hide her trembling lips and the tears that slide down her cheeks. I felt so badly for what she read about her mom and hoped that I could fill her day with happiness as we prepared for our nuptials.

Chapter 7
OUR NUPTIALS

Finally, our long-awaited wedding day had arrived. It could not have been a more specular beginning to the day as I peeked out the bedroom windows. Bright early morning sun and a gentle breeze blew in off the ocean. With excitement "Yes," came flying out of my mouth.

Patrick had spent the night in town with his groomsmen while my bridesmaids had spent the evening with me at the house, in part for fun and camaraderie for which I was grateful. We shared many stories of the old days and laughed as we remembered the crazy things we used to do.

My dad and Liv had awakened early to prepare breakfast for all of us. Soon, the sound of running water from the showers and the blowing of hair dryers filled the house with an underlying murmur of voices filling the air.

A sudden obnoxious knocking at the door took me off guard as we were not expecting visitors until later in the morning. Annoyed, I answered the front door and was shocked to see Sharon standing there with a small gift of offering in her hands. My mind spun like a top wishing she and they would just go away.

"We just wanted to wish you well on your special day." She said.

I thanked her as I wondered if she was regifting one of the presents she may have stolen. Sharon turned her head toward the end of the driveway, I stuck my head out of the door to see what she was looking at. There was Steven and Jonathan going for their morning stroll. A wave was exchanged between us, and I couldn't help but wonder if this would be the only intrusion that we would have from them today.

Sharon took several steps forward edging herself towards the open door. She was eyeing the inside of the house looking into every corner that was visible. Another step closer suggested that she was looking for an invitation to enter. I was in my bath robe and not at all ready to engage with her. I thanked her again and made an excuse to withdraw back inside to my company. I felt badly but at the same time I didn't trust this woman in anyway and always felt she had an ulterior motive.

The hours began to move quickly and soon I found myself putting on my wedding gown. Butterflies filled each of our bellies as we pretended to be busy, just waiting.

Patrick arrived shortly before noon along with the band, caterers, and a few groomsmen. We watched from the second-floor windows where there seemed to be a disturbance near the arbor. Several of Patrick's friends addressed the problem when I heard Tony say, "All is well. I've got this!"

Tony and Patrick had been friends for many years and he was one of our groomsmen. His wife Debbie was a justice of the peace and would be officiating at our wedding.

Tony was always jovial, the proverbial jokester and the life of every party, so when I heard the concern in his voice, I could not help but wonder if that old scruffy dog had found his way into the backyard disturbing the gardens again. I banished the thought and focused on the excitement to come.

My maid of honor, Jan, helped me with my veil as it was near time to leave for the church. Limousines arrived within 15 minutes, and we were whisked away. By the time we arrived at the small cathedral the groomsmen and Patrick were standing in front of the alter and every pew was filled.

Debbie, Justice of the Peace was a dark-haired woman with an explosive personality and eyes that expressed every emotion fully. I had known Debbie for years but never had the time or opportunity to bond with her as we were at various stages of life. Never did I expected to see her here at this little church in the middle of nowhere. However, I quickly learned that she had planned to surprise us by officiating at our wedding from the moment she knew Pat and I were getting married. Debbie was astounding and put my mind at ease. She took care of all the church details, scripture, passages and even had ideas for our vows, yet Patrick and I had written our own vows and were comfortable with what we wanted to say to one another.

Over the months leading up to the wedding she and I became fast friends sharing our life stories and getting to know one another on a more intimate level. I told her I had lost my mom several years ago giving her what minute details I had. Somehow, she stepped up to the plate filling in all the tasks that mothers take on during such an important day.

As I stood in the small vestibule of the church filled with chatter, a sudden ominous silence befell the cathedral-like room. Debbie had taken her place on the alter. Music began to play and I on my father's arm began the walk toward Patrick. His eyes were filled with tears, as his broad illuminated smile captured my heart, revealing the happiness he felt.

Debbie read each scripture with a guiding tone as if to warn us to hold true to the vows we were taking. Her most important word was, 'listen,' do not talk. Take words in, think about them before you ever respond. This was a lesson for each of us to ponder.

"I now pronounce you man and wife." She announced.

We sealed our vows with a kiss. High fives and a roar from the guests sealed our fate. As our guests left the church, they formed a line in front of the cobble stoned walkway, and we happily welcomed each of them for coming to honor our special day. At the end of the line was Sharon, Steven and Jonathan standing there with twisted smiles on their faces. Patrick awkwardly thanked them for stopping by and graciously apologized reminded them that they had not been invited to the festivities at the house. It was his hope that they got the message.

Other well-wishers tooted their horns and Debbie released bouquets of balloons in celebration of our union. Ferron and Olivia guided us away from the awkward interference of our neighbors, making small talk to divert our departure. My stomach turned as nausea and a watery mouth took over my body. I refused to let those odd people ruin my day but could not help but wonder what else they had in store for us.

⟋∞ THE RECEPTION ∞⟍

Blue skies and a gentle breeze mixed with music and the smell of fragment flowers graced our backyard. We arrived in time to see the bar filled with those wishing to begin a buzz to last the night away. Trays of hors d'oeuvres were being served by our caterers and raves of appreciation were whispered throughout the crowd. We only had what seemed moments until the band announced our names as Mr. and Mrs. Stone, beckoning us to the floor for our first dance. Soon, everyone joined us, as the party began.

Debbie arranged with the musicians that they play a special wedding song, which brought everyone to their feet. Hands were clasped and held high above our heads as men on each end of the line swirled their handkerchiefs in a wild circle. Their feet were crossed, and knees bent as they kicked up their heels bringing on a roar of excitement from the participants.

Tony raised his glass giving the first of several toasts. We laughed at the jokes told of our secret life events and continued enjoying every moment of the afternoon.

My father tearfully said words of congratulations bringing on tears from many who knew of my mother's death and the sadness my father had lived until this special event. We could not have been happier than to see the joy that Liv had brought to my dad and hoped beyond hope that their relationship would last forever.

The afternoon soon slid into evening as the festivities began to wind down. The view of the sun setting over the horizon was magnificent, making many sad to leave as our guests began their journey into the town to be near the ferry for an early morning departure. We said our goodbyes with hugs and kisses, promising to catch up after the honeymoon.

Dad, Liv, Jan, and Tony stayed on to oversee the clean-up crew the next day. We sat reminiscing about how wonderful everything went and could not help but mention the house on the hill and how the Samuels and Jonathan thankfully stayed far away from the reception, although they were seen gawking from their front porch at the festivities in our yard. If that was the worst of it, we considered ourselves lucky.

By nine am we had left for the airport to begin our honeymoon, leaving the rest to fend for themselves.

Devin started the coffee pot as Liv prepared a simple breakfast. Jan, with breakfast in hand had taken to the outside patio for a breath of fresh air, when a sudden flock of ravens came swooping down into the backyard squawking loudly as they landed on the beautiful flower garden. They were frenzied, as the pecked wildly at the ground. Jan called for the others to come outside, Devin and Tony waved the bird away by making noise and throwing rocks at them. The flock flew straight up into the sky, hovering for a brief time then swooping back down invading the entire yard. Jan supposed that many crumbs made their way to the ground from the night before as well as the food she had taken outside for her breakfast. She let the thought of the invasion go, hoping they would fly away as quickly as they had appeared.

A sudden shift in the winds brought the stench of rotting food that filled the entire neighborhood with a foul odor. Jan panicked when she noticed a handful of turkey vultures began circling above.

"What the hell is going on? Someone, please help me! Help! Frantically, she screamed as several ravens began pecking at her head. Devin opened the back sliders and sent a long blow from the foghorn out into the atmosphere, scaring the birds away momentarily. It was nothing less than a nightmare or a scene from Alfred Hitchcock's 'The Birds.'

Hunter Richardson had arrived with him cleanup crew. Each of the workers complained of a stench permeating the area. Hunter took Devin aside and in a quiet tone explained that the pungent smell seeping into the neighborhood was not of rotten food but was that of human decomposition. Immediately, Devin followed Hunter towards the back garden where the birds had landed pecking at the flower beds. Hunter told Pat of his history and how during his college days worked for the coroner's office which revealed his knowledge of the smell of decay.

Jan was listening from afar and decided to exam the garden bed for herself. A sudden scream rose into the atmosphere alerting Pat and Hunter that she needed help. They arrived at her side in time to see her faint dead away right on top of the garden. Tony called EMS however and when they arrived Jan refused to go with them to the Emergency Center for a more thorough examine. Instead, she decided it best to examine the area more carefully in doing so, she found fingers sticking up through the dirt stiff and black from rot. Six feet away was a black leather shoe approximately size twelve protruding from the garden.

A call was placed to 911 and the men stood vigil near the death site making certain the area was not compromised.

Chapter 8
A RESTING PLACE

❦ DEVIN'S VOICE ❦

Within moments sirens were blaring. Six cruisers came flying over the hillside. Officers, detectives with the coroner's staff in tow. The police knew the history of the problem neighbors above us and of their dog that always found his way into Patrick and Haley's Garden. Simultaneously, they sent detectives to the house on the hill. Yet again I notice that no one answered the door.

My daughter and Patrick's house was a buzz as Jan and Tony tried to explain to the officers what had happened that morning regarding the onslaught of birds and horrible odor coming from the back garden. The detectives were taking notes furiously while others walked the perimeter of the property looking for evidence.

We realized there were suspicions that the body in the garden could be that of Constable Harrison, as to date he still has not been heard from. We over-heard the detectives saying that Harrison's cruiser had been found half submerged about one mile down the coastline. Weeks in salt water destroyed any usable evidence. They surmised that the vehicle had been pushed over the cliffs smashing into the rocks then pulled by the strong waves and currents, resting on one of the many rocky cliffs below.

It was hard to conceive that the Samuels, an elderly couple in poor health could have possibly pushed the vehicle into the ocean, yet Olivia's account of the couple's ill health screamed of lies and the faking of Mr. Samuels infirmities.

Another warrant was issued for the Samuel home. It was the story told by Olivia Michaels that spurred the inquisition and interest in the old couple. Earlier fingerprints had been taken of both husband and wife, which led nowhere. There were no previous prints on file for Mrs. or Mr. Samuels as Steven's fingertips and palm prints had been burnt off in a fire some years ago. Due to the recent break- ins at the Stone house Sharon's prints were now on record but there was no way of telling if she was the only perpetrator.

The Police discovered that there was no valid marriage license for the Samuels and surmised that they were living together in a common law arrangement.

All the guests had left for home; leaving Liv and Devin to hold the fort until the newlyweds returned home from their honeymoon.

∞ AFTER THE HONEYMOON ∞

"As soon as Haley and Pat arrived home Liv and I carefully explained the situation and all the police findings to the both of them. They were shocked to learn that Constable Harrison was found dead in their own garden. Everything was beginning to make sense in an odd way. The Scruffy old dog continued to return to the garden and Sharon's meddling, and constant surveillance of our property via the telescope remained unchanged. But, why? Who were those very odd people and why had they chosen my daughter and her husband to harass?"

"The investigation of the Samuels home went on for weeks, until finally it was revealed that yes, the blood found in the house on the hill was that of both Constable Harrison and Olivia Michaels. The coroner's report concluded that it was the body of Constable Harrison, and his cause of death was from blunt force trauma to the back of his head, certainly confirming it was a homicide. An immediate APB was put out for the Samuels, yet they had disappeared. The police were feverish in a quest to find the couple on the hill.

Sadly, the family of James Harrison waited an agonizing three weeks before arrangements could be made for his funeral. He served his community for twenty-five years with honor and in good standing. A Veteran, he served in the U.S. army, his reputation was stellar. James was respected and would be sorely missed. We all felt it necessary to attend the services to pay our respects to his family and the police department because, if it weren't for our request that an officer come to our house that fateful day, he would still be alive. Guilt was haunting the newlyweds.

The day after the funeral the police were banging at our front door first thing in the morning. They needed to speak with Haley and me as we were still trying to digest all that had occurred during our absence. The police were relentless in their aggressive questioning of everyone including the Michaels, whom they interviewed separately. They insisted on knowing everything from the time each of the parties had moved into the neighborhood and of their relationships with the Samuels.

The police alluded to the fact that they questioned the honestly of the Michaels as for some unknown reason they raised suspicion with the answers they gave."

Haley found that to be improbably, she trusted Olivia and Ferron and had high

hopes that they were wrong in their summation of the Doctor and his wife. Haley considered them to be close friends. Yet, on second thought she agreed that they were modestly aggressive in there meeting and friendship of she and Patrick. They had never once been invited to the Michael's home and wondered why.

Haley told the police of the break-ins by Sharon and the disarray of her wedding gifts. She also mentioned that Olivia had told her of the telescope on the third floor where Mr. Samuels would spy on the Stone family. Initially the police suggested that they were just a senile old couple and harmless, yet this investigation was quickly taking a turn in a vastly different direction. Haley continued telling the officers of the frequent impromptu visits made by the Michaels and of Olivia's employment with the Samuel's family. Immediately, the police checked out Olivia's story that she was employed by a healthcare company in town. It turned out that she was not an employee of any company and that she solicited that job on her own; or did she?

"Why would she lie to either one of us? That makes no sense."

The police turned their attention to Ferron and Olivia spending hours at their home increasingly asking more questions. We were not present and knew nothing of their telling but had hopes that they would be truthful.

At that point Patrick asked some of the agents from his office to begin delving into Maddie Morgan's case, he requested that they contact the Mallory Cove police department. The agents were on top of it. It was only a few days before word came from Lieutenant Kevin Dillon and Detective Diane George who were happy to have the FBI inquiring into the Morgan case, which, had been dormant for too many years. The two police officers from Mallory Cove had interviewed everyone who had attended Maddie's funeral. They found many had suspicions about John Stone and some had stories that would turn heads regarding Maddie's promiscuous behavior with many men in their town. She had no shame and would boast of her insatiable sexual appetite. On several occasions, the name Father Dario Diaz came up suggesting that Maddie would often visit him in the rectory of his church. It was not known if she was repenting her sins or getting counseling for her marital issues or if there was a more sinister reason for her visits. Maddie was not one who could be trusted even in the presence of a priest.

It would take time before they received any news from Mallory Cove. It was then time to wait on evidence to arrive from Wisconsin and focus on what could be learned from the professionals on the Vineyard.

Devin and Liv were staying in town for several days meeting with realtors as they looked for prospects of a new home in the area. It was the perfect time for Haley and Patrick to search their mothers' diaries for any clues they might reveal.

Chapter 9
MADDIE'S DIARY

It was a bleak rainy day; thunder and lightning persisted throughout the entire afternoon lending itself to nestling into big comfy chairs to read. It was our hope that we would find answers that would unravel the deaths of our mothers and shed light on what the hell, was going on.

⟩∞ MADDIE'S DIARY ∞⟨

The phenomenon of Indian summer was upon us that year in late November, with temperatures in the late seventies. I decided it was the perfect day to take the 'Princess' out for one more sail. Golan Lake was sparkling that day and I thought it was the right time to try to renew our broken friendship.

Sam had prepared a fabulous lunch with lots of wine, sandwiches and hors d' oeuvres to offer. I tried to make small talk and asked about she and John's pending divorce. Immediately, I was met with silence and a cold hard stare. Sam was livid and I for the life of me couldn't understand why. For god's sake we had been best friends since childhood. I surmised that she had suspicions about me due to my lifestyle of promiscuity and yes, I did feel some guilt, but for her to treat me that way when I was only trying to be kind truly sent me over an edge. How could she have possible known that I was screwing John too?

I knew she had found John's scarf wreaking of his cologne in the back office at Morgana Design the first day I had taken her there. She also found Photos of me having sex with a friend whose body was buffed to the max and free from body hair. The thought of him still turns me on all these years later. Sure, I was embarrassed but it wasn't any of her business. Sam was always so anxious, I often wondered if she ever had an orgasm. Maybe, that was why John strayed.

Our time on the water was going well when suddenly, I was overtaken with jealousy, rage, and hatred. How, in god's name did Sam hook John? What was so special about that ridged bitch? Did I have too much wine? Somehow, I wanted to hurt her and with that I let the boom fly free sending Sam into the deep icy waters of the lake. I meant to do it and that one action made me feel powerful. And yes, I rammed the grappling pole into her gut hoping she would drown. If she hadn't been rescued by two-jet skiers, I would have accomplished my mission.

Haley sat shocked at her mother's own words. Tears fell from her eyes as her stomach churned. As painful as it was to read this confession, she knew the answers where right there in front of her.

⊃✕ EXCERPT TWO ✕⊂

I knew of Sam's meetings with her psychologist Dr. Steven Silverman in New York. And I made it my mission to learn all I could about why Sam had a need for the doctor's services. There was a glitch in Sam's program, and I knew that one little secret kept me from knowing who Sam really was. No one in the world could live such a pure life and I was compelled to find out the truth one way or another.

I was proud of my self that I still had the ability to persuade anyone with temptations of a sexual nature. Steven was an easy mark and was perverted just like me. I never understood why the good doctor was infatuated with Sam, yet he was and badly so. He would often tell me what he would do to her if he could get close enough to her, it turned me on, and I found myself saturated with desire.

Steven was very handsome and strong, but he was odd in ways I couldn't imagine. It was if he were hiding something and as I tried to dig information out of him, he would withdraw becoming aloof. At first, I thought it was because he was a doctor and held true to the rules of confidentiality and I quickly learned that my prodding was at a dead end.

Humm, a new hire was on the payroll at Morgana Design, left me shocked. Devin took on a stranger to clean up after certain building sites. Jerod Deaver's apparently made a deal with Devin that he would be able to stay in the back room, use the shower and cook his breakfast there as he looked for a permanent place to stay. After a time, I met Jerod and found there was a familiarity to him, one I could not put my finger on. His body was firm, he was five'11" and his face looked as though it had been surgically altered. Immediately, I dashed the thought that I could have known him.

⟨⟩ EXCERPT THREE ⟨⟩

I am frightened. Someone follows me in a dark colored car with tinted windows leaving me with an eerie feeling. I made sure to be vigilant yet, it seemed, that eyes followed me everywhere. Weeks later, the tires on my vehicle had been slashed in my own garage. How could that be? I was constantly watching my own back. Was it someone's wife who found out that I had been having an affair with her husband and thought I would spill the beans ruining their life together? Dear god, this insane lifestyle was beginning to catch up with me and fear gripped my soul. I was a great liar and hid everything from Devin successfully, or at least I believed that to be true.

⟨⟩ EXCERPT FOUR ⟨⟩

I saw the way that Sam would look at Devin. I felt, she had a crush on him although she never would have admitted that to me. After the sailing trip and Sam's near drowning I saw the way he took care of her, leaving me to fend for myself. In his heart of hearts, I knew he hated me. He knew I was a liar and cheat, but I don't think he knew it was a sickness that I couldn't wrap my own mind around.

The day I had taken Samantha to the airport for the twin's graduation she threw a handful of photos, the scarf that belonged to John and other evidence she had been collecting for months right in my face. When I tried to explain things to her, she already was out of the car, I met her on the passenger sidewalk, but she was not having it and knocked me to the ground.

"I'll take care of you when I get back, then you'll have a lot of explaining to do." Sam said.

"Enough!!" flew out of my mouth. My mother was as sick as they come and all these years, I thought she was a jewel of society. I was so wrong and disappointed, broken to the core. I slammed the diary closed nearly ripping off the cover as I hollered through the house trying to find Patrick.

I found him in the garden area where he sat overlooking the ocean. His mother's diary was in his hands and his head hung over his knees. I approached easily and asked him what he had read?"

We agreed that much of what I told him of my mother's writing was confirmed with what his mother had disclosed in her diary. But still that was no reason for any of what had happened leaving a blank that needed to be filled in. Patrick said his mother insisted that her friend Maura had all the answers as she was Sam's confidant while all the mysteries were unraveling. Patrick thumbed through the diary and found Maura's old phone number and address near the last page.

"We have to call her Haley, maybe she'll have some answers."

They took a moment to catch their breath. Patrick continued to explain to Haley that in his mother's diary, he read that there had been a fire in the house while Sam was home alone. Mom told how she lent her car to Maddie because all her tires had been slashed with a knife. Maddie needed to go to the office that day and Mom said yes, allowing her to borrow mom's car, which allowed Sam to work from the Morgan's home office that day.

"Although my mother was angry with Maddie, she made dinner for them both, yet Maddie never came home. I believe, that was the night that Maddie died. Perhaps, she was drunk or driving too fast as originally alleged. Mom wrote that the break lines on the vehicle had been cut. And eventually the police called the incident a homicide.

Together she and Devin, who was absolutely destroyed by Maddie's death took care of all the funeral arrangements and saw the entire family through that tough time. It was a nightmare of epic proportions, which left so many unanswered questions, as we both remember."

"Yes, it was horrific." Tears fell from Haley's eyes.

Patrick had so much compassion and empathy for Haley as he had lived the nightmare too.

"There was a part in my mom's writing that told of an encounter she had with a man she met on the plane. He found her in Boston, but it seemed to me, that he followed her to the Hilton and whisked her off to dinner and then to his offbeat hotel to have a sexual escapade. She was afraid but was sick of being so nervous about being with another man, she let her guard down and regretted their consummation."

"Devin? Please get Maura's number and let's call now, we can not continue to play guessing games here."

Our hearts were beating feverishly as the phone rang on the other end. It took several minutes for someone to answer.

"Hello?"

"Hello. Ma'am. I'm looking for Maura McNeal Vogt."

"Yes, that's me. How can I help you?"

"I don't know quite how to begin. My name is Johnny Stone the son of Samantha Stone, but now I use my middle name Patrick. Do you recall my mother's name?"

Dead silence met Patrick as he waited for an answer. Had he made a mistake to call this woman he only vaguely remembered? Then a burst of excitement rang through the phone.

"Yes, I well remember your mother. She and I were the best of friends for many years, and I worked as a forensic nurse on your mother's case. I have missed her every day since her passing. How can I help you?"

"Well, Maura I have just recently married Haley Morgan, we are living out on Martha's Vineyard now. As a gift from Devin Morgan, both Haley and I were given the diaries that Maddie and Sam had kept; neither of their cases were ever closed and to date they remain cold case files in Mallory Cove. We are looking for the truth of what had happened. In my mother's diary there was a suggestion that you may have many of the answers we are looking for. We have been reading each of their writings but need clarity on most everything we found. Are you able to help us in any way?"

Again, there was a long silence on the end of the phone and Patrick stomach dropped thinking they had hit a dead end. Finally, after a long void came a mumble of resignation, as Maura began to speak.

"I have been holding on to secrets that need to be told before I pass away, or all will be lost forever. What I tell you, may be hard to hear, and I too will be admitting to guilt. Please forgive me, before I even begin."

Haley was listening on the other line and we both shuddered to think the answers were here all the time. How could the police have missed such an important witness in Maura?

Tears came easily, as Maura had difficulty composing herself. Sniffles and a nose blow with deep sighs filled the air waves in repetition. Together, Haley and I wondered the reason she was so upset, twenty years, after my mom's death?

"I had taken care of your mom shortly after she was admitted into the hospital." At that time, I worked as a forensic nurse. It was thought by many, that I would be

able to find the answers to unravel the mystery of your mother's illness. Sadly, forensics were not as they are today, and I felt so much guilt that I failed your mom and both you and Julieann."

"Please don't beat yourself up over this, it's just that we need answers as to what exactly happened. We need to understand Maddie and Sam's relationship as there seemed to be a deep seeded problem between them. It seemed that the two of them had suitors who wanted to do them harm. But why?"

Suddenly, Maura asked if it would be possible that she visit them on the Vineyard as she had something particularly important to give to Patrick.

Excitedly, they both screamed out, "yes."

"We would be more than happy to have you here. When can you come out our way?"

"I would like to come as soon as possible if you don't mind. I will look for airline tickets this evening and give you a call back."

Maura then reiterated Patrick's phone number making certain she had it correctly.

"Good-bye for now, I'll be in touch tomorrow."

Chapter 10
MAURA'S CONFESSION

The phone rang by late evening and Maura gave her arrival time, date, and airline on which she would be traveling. Patrick's face turned pale wondering what news Maura would reveal. Fear ripped through him unsure if he genuinely wanted to hear the answers to his many questions. Then, Maura unexpectedly began to tell what she knew.

"I was Sam's best friend for many years stemming from our childhood. I'm not sure if you remember me and Carl from our days in Connecticut?"

"Of course, I do Patrick said. And I well remember you from Maddie's funeral. You were so kind to all the children in attendance back then."

"Patrick, I was also your mom's confidant throughout the divorce proceedings and during the time she spent with Maddie and Devin. As Sam drove the long miles from the airport when she first arrived in the mid-west, I would keep her company by phone, and it was then that I learned about what had been happening in her life. I know that she and your dad had many issues and she had become afraid of him as she watched his transition from a loving husband filled with kindness and compassion into one who was obsessed with sexual deviance, rage, and control issues.

What I'm telling you may be somewhat brutal for you to hear, but Sam would want you to know the truth. So, I am sorry beforehand. She felt he had taken his frustrations out on you and Julieann and that was unacceptable to her on every level. She never wanted either of you to feel his wrath or get used to the abuse he would dish out. Sam came to a point where she needed her freedom back, to do as she chose. She had a longing desire to return to the work force and feel as though she was a contributor to society, something your dad had taken away from her.

There was a point where she tried so hard to make it work, yet she was met with his resistance at every turn. I believe he didn't want the situation to improve which left your mother sad and in despair.

It was at that point that she accepted the offer made by Maddie to go to Wisconsin and begin a new life. She also called her lawyer Paulette Winslow to begin divorce proceeding, which did not initially sit well with John."

"Maddie was very promiscuous and always had been throughout their college days, but Sam felt she could manage Maddie. Turned out that Sam had suspicions about Maddie having an affair with your father. She was sickened by this revelation and stood back from Maddie. Sam stayed on, in Mallory Cove only to fulfill her obligation to complete an internship with Morgana Design. Her intent was to finish as soon as she could and move back to Westport to begin her own business.

Sam never did anything to deserve any of what was dished out to her. I felt so helpless, but all I could do was just listen and I did.

She told me of the sail on Golan Lake and how Maddie intentionally tried to drown her. I was shocked that she would stay on at that point, but Sam bought a gun that she held close to her as she watched Maddie's every move. That Christmas you and Julieann headed out to visit your mom. Sam was filled with joy and hoped Maddie would get over her issues of jealousy with her.

She also told me of the night the three of you went to the movies in Ducks Landing and of the car that nearly ran you off the road and the other car that nearly took Julieann's life. Something was very wrong, and your mom had a bit of investigator in her as well, having extrasensory perception and all. She felt it necessary to solve the mystery by herself. A million times I told her to give it up and get the hell out of there before something sinister happened.

It wasn't long after, that Maddie died in a car accident. It was called a murder as the break lines had been cut nearly in half making her lose control of the vehicle."

I was with Sam at the funeral along with friends from Westport. We watched your father harass her as he intruded on Devin and others returning to the house on Newcomb Drive. It was awful, but your mom oversaw it well. Devin finally, spoke with his father who had the courage to ask John to find a place to stay in town. John's ego was enraged as he couldn't believe that he was not the center of anyone's attention.

Prior to the funeral by two weeks there was an explosion at the house and the fire destroyed the back-office area leaving the place a mess. Luckily, the insurance company was able to fix it enough so that after the funeral services were held, we were able to return to the house where family and friends could gather in the unaffected areas.

"Patrick, I must continue speaking to you when we are together it is all too much to tell in a phone conversation. Maura's abrupt end to their conversation surprised Patrick, leaving him bewildered.

"Goodnight, Patrick, I'll see you on Wednesday." Stunned, Patrick said his goodnight with tears in his eyes and a fallen heart as he knew there was so much to learn in the week to come.

The next few days took Haley and Patrick back to their diaries as they search for anything to corroborate what Maura had told him. And yes, it was affirmed that many of the scenarios told by Maura where right there in their own mother's handwriting.

A few days later Maura arrived on time and was whisked away by a limo that met her at Martha's Vineyard Airport. From the back patio we could see the limo's front fender push its way over the hill heading directly towards our home. Haley and I made our way to the driveway where we welcomed Maura. She was delighted to see us and acclaimed that Sam would have been thrilled at our success and union. After some refreshments we went to work trying to unravel the mysteries of our mom's deaths. Both Haley and I shook with fear of what we were about to learn.

Maura seemed to want to get right to the nitty gritty as if a cleansing of the soul was in order. She began by telling of the night in the hospital when she recognized a visitor who had been in Sam's room. Her suspicions were aroused as she recognized his deformed right arm from a severe break he received in an accident when he was a kid. She questioned the mystery man on his way out and decided that he was her long-lost brother, Cathal McNeal an ex-con who had been at odds with their family for years. Cathal never returned to the family when our dad passed away and that on its own was an unforgivable offense. It was revealed sometime later that he was in prison at the time.

"Look, I know you may blame me for keeping this all from you and I don't blame you for that, but I was in the dark like everyone else. As the years past, I started putting two and two together and suddenly it was as if a light turned on. I learned that Cathal started studying psychology while in prison and received his Bachelors' degree while there. When he got out, he opened his own office and was seeing private patients in New York City, something that was against the conditions of his release from prison. Cathal always lived on the edge testing everyone's patience as he broke every rule in the book. He was able to fool everyone for a long time by using the names of many of his cellmates. Aliases were his thing, that way he stayed one step ahead of the law. I presume?"

"Do you recognize names such as Jerad Devers, or Jaden Donaldson? Do you remember them?" Patrick asked.

"Cathal favored names with the letters JD, however I don't recognize any of those names. Why do you ask Patrick?"

"Those names were found in the diaries that my dad gave to us."

"I do, however, remember the name of Jason Davis a gentleman she met on the airplane as she flew back into Connecticut for the divorce proceedings. I must confess that I believe, Jason Davis is another alias used by Cathal as a disguise. And to add insult to injury I believe, Jason Davis and all the other JD names were used, by my brother. For all these years I have felt so very guilty about all of this, but I was afraid of repercussions from Cathal. Now, I just want everything in the open and to find out for sure if this is true, enough time has been wasted and no-one has any answers. Please forgive me for not coming forth sooner."

Haley and Patrick sat dumb founded in silence as they tried to digest what Maura had told them, tears streamed from their eyes and Patrick had difficulty holding his tongue.

"Do you have a photo of Cathal that we can see?" Haley asked.

"Yes of course, here, look at this." Maura fumbled in her purse digging into all the compartments until finally, she stretched out her long slender arm and said. "Here you go, I hope this helps. I should also tell you that I believe that Cathal has had plastic surgery through the years, again his way of avoiding capture."

As Patrick looked at the photo, he gasped recognizing Cathal as Dr. Steven Silverman, the same man that both he and his mother had trusted. They were the same or they certainly looked like twins. The man in the photo also resembled the old man on the hill above them. Patrick immediately went for his phone and called his friends at the FBI to do a check of the man whose photo he held in his hands.

"Maura, I know how difficult this must be for you and I thank you for your courage in coming here to explain what you know of the case."

"Please know, Patrick, that I only surmise this to be true, but certainly more investigation must be done. I have one more thing to offer here. Maura slid her hand in her pocket and pulled out a key, then reaching into a gym bag she pulled out a small glass box then slid the key into the lock and reached inside, here this is for you. A clump of strawberry blonde hair was placed into Patrick's large hands. Yes, I took your mother's hair out of her head by the roots the day she lay dying, hoping that one day someone could run forensics on it to see what kind of poison was used to kill her.

I tried to have it evaluated but at the time DNA was new and my friend Kojak with the state police needed to have permission from your father to have any testing done.

In other words, a case number had to be assigned to the evidence presented. That would have enraged John leaving me next on his list of knock-offs. Besides, he had disappeared right after your mom's cremation."

"But why didn't he just divorce her? This makes no sense that he would go to such an extreme and be on the run for the rest of his life."

"Money, Patrick it's all about the money. Kojak was able to tell me that John had several large insurance policies out on Sam's life that would leave him all set forever. Not only that, but your mom was left two different inheritances from her grandfather and an old spinster aunt who loved Sam dearly. Your father stood to claim everything when she died."

'That son of a bitch! How could he do such a thing? This is unbelievable, unbelievable! If only I could get my, hands- on him. So, what was Cathal's roll in all this?"

"Cathal, was hired by John, to keep an eye on Sam. The problem with that, is that my brother was a rapist who fell in love with Sam and refused to leave her alone. He had troubles from his youth that followed him throughout his life. Cathal knew Sam as we were all neighbors back in Westport during our youth, but he was ten years younger than us and although handsome he was easily forgotten, spending lots of time in Juvie.

A divorce from John would have negated him on any monies he may have inherited,

plus, any of the insurances he would have collected. It is my understanding that he did collect on some money, but the police suspicions put a hold on several other documents for which he received nothing.

Lieutenant Kevin Dillion of the Mallory Cove police department informed me that through the years there had been attempts to claim the policy money. However, they were never able to find out who it was that was making the claims. Always offshore accounts under false names and false attorneys."

Maura was feeling satisfied with the results and progress of the case and with Haley and Patrick's permission she decided to stay on until the mystery was solved. She was more than ready to testify against her brother if it came to that.

Chapter Eleven
FINDING THE TRUTH

H aley and I were shocked to realize that through the years headway was made in our mothers' cases, yet no one bothered to inform us of any progress.

I was certain that between the different police agencies involved that we would uncover the truth. Sadly, the wait was on. A meeting with all agencies who had worked on our cases through the years was called. By Monday morning we sat around a large oak conference table at the Martha's Vineyard police station. Each person involved told what they knew but this was the first time that all the information was coming together in one place.

Mallory Cove police added that there were suspicions regarding Cathal having an affair with Maddie and in turn Maddie was sexually involved with John, which made her collateral damage. Jerod Deaver's, aka, Cathal cut the brake lines on Sam's car, which Maddie had borrowed from Sam the day of her death, sending Maddie spinning out of control as she careened down the windy rain-soaked road sending her into the thicket of trees, which ended her life. It was new forensics from hair follicles that put Cathal at the Morgana Design Center. It is not certain that Maddie's death was the intent of all this planning or if Sam was the intended target of misfortune. From John's aloofness and his reaction at the funeral it was difficult to read what his responsibility or roll in the accident may have been. Some of our friends remembered him saying."

"It seemed, that the wrong women died." John said. And that was enough to seal his involvement in Maddie's death as many contended.

MALLORY COVE INFORMATION

Maura told of the house fire on Newcomb Drive, and the fact that Sam also reported she had been raped and made a trip into the ER in Ducks Landing to preserve the evidence. After all these years DNA is bringing everything full circle as forensics has advanced into a science of its own.

Suddenly, the MV captain jumped in stating that the Harrison case was their first priority to investigate. Once complete they would take on the cold case file for the Stone family.

"Our focus is to find the Samuels and hold them accountable for the death of James Harrison because we have no idea who they really are, perhaps one thing will lead to another."

The meeting was adjourned, and the search began throughout New England and the U.S. to bring these fugitives to justice.

Not more than a week into the search did the police locate the Samuels in New York right back in their old neighborhood. It was an easy find and the police had enough of a circumstantial case to charge them both with homicide in the death of Constable Harrison. Mr. Samuels was defiant and verbally abusive when taken into custody. Sharon on the other hand was meek and visually nervous. When alone she told one of the officers that she wanted to make a deal as she could no longer carry the burden of all the secrets from the past. In the interrogation room Sharon Samuels was asked her name.

"My name is Melissa Connors."

"Where did the name Sharon come from?"

"It was a name made up by Jason Davis aka Dr. Silverman also known as Cathal McNeal. You must understand that you can never say no to Cathal in any way. He is sick and I easily could have become one of his victims."

"Continue from the beginning." The officer demanded.

"Years ago, we all met in Westport, Connecticut where we lived and worked. I was young then and was coerced into becoming a drug representative for an unknown company headed by John Stone. He was a chemist and was single handedly producing illicit drugs in his lab at the university.

Cathal and I sold those drugs throughout the United States. Making John an extraordinarily rich man. Early on, John retained and set him up as a psychiatrist in New York City and insisted his wife and son go to him so that Cathal could keep an eye on the both of them. He did not want her to find out what he was doing as she would divorce him leaving his personal life in ruins. As I hear it, John destroyed himself by becoming an addict and in that, he became a sexual fiend. I was used as part of his scheme in many ways."

"Why didn't he just divorce Sam?"

"John had a huge ego and wanted it all. You could never suggest or attempt to tell John what or how to do anything, that was unheard of, and he would easily take his rath out on anyone who stood in his way."

In a separate interrogation room Steven Samuels was being questioned, yet he refused to speak with anyone and insisted on awaiting the arrival of his New York guru Attorney Dominic Torino to show up on the small island. Steven was then taken into custody and charged with first degree murder. He stood up turned around, was cuffed then led away. The police were shocked at his request because at first, he refused counsel and the police thought perhaps he had enough of the insane life he had been living. Sadly, he seemed to have been born to live a life of crime and destruction.

In room (2) Sharon explained how Steven had hit Harrison in the head several times taking him down because he was afraid to be exposed for the criminal he was and at his age prison would not agree with him. Together they dragged him out of the house and during the night they rolled him down the hill to the Stones perfect garden for burial. Later that night, in the wee hours of the morning they dressed in black, released the brakes on the police cruiser and pushed the vehicle into the ocean from the high cliffs of their home. Sharon then stood, took a sigh of relief then turned her back on the officers, was cuffed and led away.

"It seems our case is nearly closed on the Harrison murder. Yet, there were still many more questions to be answered regarding the Michaels and how exactly they fit into the happenings at the Samuels home and why Olivia never reported being attacked when the incident occurred." Said the Captain.

Officers were sent back to the Michaels home for a more in-depth investigation. This time they had a search warrant in hand. Olivia answered the door dressed in a skimpy romper of sorts. It was as if we had disturbed a late afternoon tumble in the hay. She blushed a soft pink and flapped her long lashes as if to ward off her embarrassment. Moments later, Ferron rounded the corner of the staircase mumbling profanities as he zipped up his pants. In a stern voice he asked.

"How can we help you, again?"

His attitude sent up red flags as this no longer was the man who was obliged to assist police, instead he was irritated and seemed to be carrying a chip on his shoulders. Was it that, he was interrupted during his afternoon sexual escapade or was he harboring secrets?

"We have more questions for you Mr. Michaels and at the same time we thought that you would want to know that the Samuels have been arrested for the murder of Constable Harrison."

"Did you locate them, where were they?"

All of a sudden there was a twist in Ferron's interest in the case. His breathing quickened and his hands began to shake as his eyes darted around the room looking at the other officers who were searching their home for potential evidence.

"What the hell are you looking for? Just stop it, we have nothing to hide. So, where did you find them, he reiterated?"

"They were found in disguises at a residence in NYC. It just so happens that the condo is owned by you Mr. Michaels. Now, how could that be and what is your part in all of this?"

"I was only helping my father out. He asked me to lend my condo to a couple who are friends of his and of course, I said yes. I didn't even know who they were."

"What is the affiliation with your father? How would he know this older couple, who seem to have more secrets than anyone I have ever known?"

"Look, my father is now a wealthy man. I never knew him growing up but when he says jump, I ask how high. He had been in prison for most of my life. Within the past five years we reconnected. I do what I can to please him so that we can maintain a relationship."

"What is your father's name?"

"He has changed his name since those days, but he was known as Jaden Donaldson during his troubled years. He came to me about a year ago asking me to purchase this home so that he could live with us. In a brief time, we relocate here on the Vineyard. Of course, we thought it might be an innovative idea to do some island living with me being in oceanography, it was the perfect place for us to settle. I found a job at Woods Hole and the rest is history."

"Knowing your father was a felon, whom you hadn't had a relationship with for all your life left you comfortable enough to have him come live with you? That doesn't make sense to me. What about you Olivia how well do you know Mr. Donaldson?"

"I had only met him on a few occasions, and he was always cordial. He suggested a job position for me taking care of an old friend of his. I thought it a bit odd that his friend happened to be our neighbor here on the Vineyard but didn't question him wanting to please both he and Ferron, so I took the job with the Samuels thinking it to be an easy harmless position."

"We need you both down at the station to make formal signed statements."

Both Ferron and Olivia were complaisant and happy to help in anyway they could which was an abrupt change of attitude from moments before. They were shocked that Mr. Donaldson knew Steven Samuels, and more delving into records revealed that Donaldson was indeed a cellmate of Cathal McNeal bringing their affiliation full circle.

The more Ferron learned of his father and his affiliation with Cathal McNeal. The more rage came from deep within him as he realized he may have been far better off, had he left his father's absence in his life a void, never to have been revisited.

Ferron had lived with his mother and had taken her birth name. He was reared properly having good manners, an excellent education and lived a crime free life unlike his biological father. He was humiliated and embarrassed to learn of his father's history of crime tainting the world as he knew it. Tears filled his eyes as he spoke with the police revealing that he would banish his father from his life once again, but this time it was on his terms. Ferron was asked why he did not know of his father's criminal history, he explained that his mother never offered the information and that in truth he didn't want to know as it may have unraveled his world at an early age.

"Sometimes it's better to walk in the dark then to face the light." He said.

∞ OLIVIA'S STATEMENT ∞

In another room Olivia answered questions regarding her job, how it came about and what her real affiliation with the Samuels was. She told how her father- in- law's suggestion to help his old friend out in his time of need would be of immense importance to him. Olivia was a bit shy and thought it to be an odd request but complied with his wishes for Ferron's sake.

She mentioned how Haley thought they were being watched via a telescope from the third-floor window of the Samuels home and how while working there she explored the third floor looking for proof to settle Haley's inquisition. She was caught red handed by Steven who attacked her drawing blood from her head and lips. Olivia also revealed how she found blood on the kitchen floor of the old man's house leading her to conclude that together he and Sharon had potentially taken the life of Constable Harrison.

In truth she had already given this information to police and had nothing else to offer this investigation. It was decided that both Olivia and Ferron were freed from any negligence in the case and were released from police custody.

On their way home they stopped by the Patrick and Haley's to find them totally absorbed in their mothers' diaries. The Michael's were forthright and told of the police inquisition and how they were exonerated for any wrongdoing, which elated Haley. The Stones began to reveal segments of their diary findings to their neighbors.

"My father treated my mother horribly for years. It is a wonder that she wanted to get as far away from him as possible. I only wish he had gotten a divorce and walked away. Apparently, his ego was too big for that. Instead, he left Julieann and me to fend for ourselves never to know the truth."

"Look here, there is a note stuck inside the pages here. It is from Liv Johnson's aunt who was our neighbor back then. Betsy Higgins describes the night that my mother tripped through the hedges in the wee hours of the morning. She and her husband Charles said mom seemed to be drunk or drugged and was speaking incoherently. My mother told them that John was trying to kill her and asked them for help. However, Charles didn't believe a word and instead of giving her refuge he handed her back over to John to continue his abuse. Only when the ambulance arrived did Charles and Betsy go over to see what had happened."

"To this day I blame myself for not having been more forceful with Charles. Sam would have been alive today if not for my weakness, said Betsy.

"And look here." Patrick flipped through the pages to reiterate Sam's account of what had happened on 'The Princess,' Maddie's sailboat, and my mothers' near drowning. I cannot believe that she went through all that garbage and still stayed on with the Morgan's. This is beyond crazy. She notes that she felt badly for Devin and wanted to finish her obligation to him for taking her in.

"That is the craziest thing I've ever heard. So, whatever happened to your father?" Ferron asked.

"It is suspect that he left the U.S. but no one knows for sure, He did an excellent job of hiding out, if in fact he's still alive."

"I have suspicions about who that old man with the scared face really is. You know the one who walks that old scruffy dog of theirs. Before I totally let loose on my father and end our relationship forever, I will ask if he knows who he might be. Perhaps its's another of their jail mates and somehow involved with this case. I feel so sorry for the both of you having to live with these mysteries for as long as you have. I promise Olivia and I will do what we can to find the answers you need."

"We just want to put all of this behind us as soon as possible so that we can live in light and a new future. Enough is enough!"

Chapter 12
THE FINAL GIFT

It had been a tumultuous week wearing on Maura, Haley, and Patrick. They were exhausted wanting the saga to end. Patrick had given his mother's hair to his forensic team for testing and after several weeks the results finally arrived by mail.

Letter from FBI's forensic team reads:

Attention Patrick Stone,

In the case of Samantha Stone, Number M-5290 it has been found in the hair follicles that both Ricin and Arsenic were of extraordinarily elevated levels, enough to have caused her death.

Arsenic, as you know is found in ground water naturally but the levels in Ms. Stone hair indicates that she had been given extrinsic amounts of poison causing seizure and eventually coma as seen in her case.

Ricin was also present in her system; it is a poison that can be found in castor beans. It can be crushed into power, pellets, or a mist.

In this case the coroner and forensic team concluded that this poison may have been administered to Ms. Stone via her nares, so as not to be visually detected. It has been determined that Samantha Stone was murdered with the said mentioned poisons.

Thank You for the opportunity to assist in this case Patrick, I hope it brings you a resolve.

Respectfully,
Luke Jones Special Agent FBI

There was dead silence as the three looked at one another in disbelief confirming what they already knew to be true. Rage filled Patrick. To relief his frustrations he spewed profanities into the air wishing his father could hear him.

"Why did all of this take so long to conclude? You Maura, had the missing link all the time and we thank you for bringing our mother's treasure to light. Now we know for sure that it was my father who laid her to rest and probably had a hand in Maddie's demise as well. His refusal to permit mom to have a Christian burial. Instead, he took it upon himself to have her remains cremated which all makes perfect sense as he showed total disrespect to her side of the family. It sickens me to think he could have done such a thing. He could have made it so much easier if he had only gotten a divorce and been done with it. Now the search must continue to bring him to justice, if in fact he is alive."

"If he is out there, we will find him as difficult as it might be, and we will make sure he gets what he has coming to him after all these years."

Maura nodded confirming her affirmation of Haley's comments.

Patrick excused himself to put a call out to Ferron leaving Maura and Haley to dig deep into their memories and into written words in Sam and Maddie's diaries as they attempted to find clues as to his whereabouts. John was very secretive about everything he did and any information about him was scarce. In truth he left a road map to nowhere, which was beyond frustrating.

Patrick needed to get to Ferron before he put questions out to his father regarding why he so coveted John and for whom he may have done such a favor. Why would Jaden expose Ferron and Olivia to the Samuels? That fact alone infuriated Ferron as his career could be ruined by his mere association with felons and criminals of any kind. He shuttered at the thought and couldn't wait to return his father's abuse and uncaring attitude. Ferron and his mother worked hard through the years to give Ferron an excellent opportunity for success and a bright future, together they superseded their own expectations.

The phone rang on the other end. Patrick waited what seemed the longest time and just as he went to hang up Ferron's mellow voice answered the call. Patrick didn't know if he had just wakened up or if he wasn't feeling well as his words were slow and exaggerated.

"Are you alright?" Patrick asked. "You sound different."

"No, I am fine, just contemplating how I want to address my father over all of this, before I throw him to the dogs once and for all."

"That's why I'm calling Ferron, we need to be together when you make your call and I need to go over a few things with you in hopes your father will provide the answers we need, would that be all right?"

Yes, that will be fine, why don't you come over in about an hour. I have to call my mother first as she will be able to tell me how best to approach him. And by the way we will refer to him as Jaden not my father. Okay? I am so upset with myself that I looked for him and attempted to have a civil relationship. I should have left it alone. Dead! We all would have been far better off."

"That will be fine, see you in a while."

Ferron showered, made himself some breakfast and nervously put a call out to his mother, hoping to find answers for both he and Patrick.

Ring, ring, "Please leave a message, I will return your call as soon as, abruptly, came a loud hello.

"I'm here. Hello, hello!"

"Mom, is that you."

"Yes baby, what's going on?"

"I have to ask you some questions about Jaden ma."

"You know that subject makes me sick. I moved on and out a long time ago."

"Yes, I know but this is important. He has potentially put me in harms way with my job and my life."

"How so Ferron?"

"This story is too long to tell now. I need to know what happened to him after your divorce. Where did he live, did he remarry, what was his life like, when did he go to prison?"

"Your father as far as I know never married again. In the beginning I thought he was a great guy, my dream come true but within the first year of being with him I found out that he was a cheat, a liar and was involved with petit crimes and carousing with other women. When he left us, he went to live with his sister Nella, who lived on a small island off the coast of Ibiza known as Formentera. His stay there was brief because he missed the big city life and the crime that was ramped here in the U.S. An apparent botched bank robbery sent him to the penitentiary."

"Who was his cellmate, do you know that?"

"I never really spoke with him after that. Years later I received a letter from your Aunt Nella telling me that a man from the United States went to live with her on the island of Formentera. Jaden had a friend who needed to hide out for a time. She surmised that he was a fugitive of some sort but never asked questions. She said he was handsome, tall, and very intelligent and she was happily having an affair with him. Your father's cellmate Cathal recommended his friend hook-up with her."

"Oh my god, thank you mom this is just what I needed, the missing links are all coming together now. I must run. I'll call you soon."

Moments later the doorbell rang, and Patrick entered with a huge mug of coffee in his hand.

"Well, my friend my mother just connected some missing links. I now know where your father ended up."

"Where? Tell me everything you know."

"He couldn't be found because he was off the coast of Spain in a place called Formentera just south of Iberia where nude beaches line the coasts. It is a small island great for hiding. Apparently, he had a relationship with my father's sister Nella who cared for him for years. He was sent there by none other than Cathal McNeal via my father, Jaden Donaldson, who was his cellmate. This is the most twisted scenario I've ever encountered. Let me call my father now that you are here and see how he explains his life away."

"Hello, Jaden here. How can I help you?"

"Jaden it's Ferron. I have some questions that I need answers to. Did you ever know a man named John Stone? Or have anything to do with him? You see I have a friend who has been missing his father for about 20 years and we think there is a link between him and your cellmate Cathal McNeal."

"Look I don't have permission to share information with you. I could get killed for doing so. I never wanted the particulars but yes, my cellmate said he had a friend who needed to disappear because he had been bouncing from place to place and was getting tired of it. The only person who lived out of the United States was my sister Nella and I recommended to them that it would be a perfect place for him to stay. Turns out they fell in love and stayed together until recently. I have no idea where he went but I do know that there was a car fire that left him horribly disfigured and depressed so Nella says. Son, I am so sorry to get you involved with any mess you may be in. The reason why I have money is because I take care of problems for many of my prison house mates. I get paid to make people disappear and I do other favors for those who need me."

"Jaden don't worry about anything. I have changed my mind about wanting any kind of relationship with you. It is over for the last time. I should have left you dead to me. Knowing you has only brought on hurt for both me and mom. You will never change and I cannot be affiliated with the likes of you. Stay away from me forever." Click!!!!

"Are you ok my friend? I know that must have been difficult but I appreciate what you've done. At least I know where my father had disappeared to. Now to find him and put him away forever."

Meanwhile Haley and Maura prepared a late lunch and awaited Patrick's return. On the back patio Maura looked toward the house on the hill and glimpsed a tall gray- haired man walking the scruffy old dog on their property. She could not see the mans face but his profile was not familiar. His height and posture seemed like the John Stone she had known so long ago. Could it be, she said under her breath?

Haley joined Maura on the patio and inquired of the old man who walked the dog.

"He is a friend of the Samuels and has been here for about a month. After Olivia had taken a beating from the old man, he showed up on the scene to assist with Steven's needs and to take care of the dog. Why do you ask?"

"Just wondering that's all. He seems somewhat familiar in an odd way. Although he is hunched over and disfigured, he looks like John Stone, Patrick's father. I wish I could get close enough to see his face."

"It isn't him, that man has spoken to Patrick on a few occasions. His face is horribly scared and disfigured and I think Patrick would have recognized his own father if that were true."

"You're probably right Haley. Sorry to bring it up."

The front door opened and Patrick excitedly went into the kitchen and directly out the back door to give Haley and Maura the good news from Ferron.

"Hey ladies, good new to bear."

"What is it, Patrick? I haven't seen you this excited for a very long time."

"Well, Ferron was able to shed light on the wear abouts of my father after all these years. It seems he Jaden, has a sister living off the coast of Spain and good ole dad has spent all these years living there, in a relationship with her."

"Are you kidding me?"

"No! that is a fact. The only thing is that apparently, he recently left there without a word to Nella, and simply disappeared. She is broken hearted I would imagine. Jaden said that John became depressed after a fire that disfigured his face and arms. He had lived with that for two years and finally was confident enough to believe that no one would recognize him. Nella has no idea where he went and neither does Ferron's mother."

Suddenly, Haley and Maura looked at one another putting two and two together as they surmised that the old man on the hill's recent appearance was more than a coincidence and the timing seemed to be right. Maura shared her concern and thoughts with Patrick. Bewildered he said he'd take a walk up the hill and confront Jonathan giving him a closer look and asking pertinent questions.

As he began to ascend the hill Patrick saw Jonathan loading up his cars and within a moment, he gunned the motor of his vehicle and was gone up over the hill, disappearing into the late afternoon clouds that ominously moved in on a heavy breeze. Patrick had missed this opportunity but was sure the old man would return for the ole scruffy dog soon.

Hours turned into days and still no one showed up at the house. The Dog could be heard barking and wailing into the night. Finally, Patrick went up the hill, banged on the door and let himself in. Jonathan, in his fury to get out of there left the door unlocked but maybe for good reason. Patrick looked around and found the house empty of photos and trivial things he had noticed on his earlier visits. The old dog was in a crate on the kitchen floor with nothing to eat or drink. A bag of dog food was near the crate and after taking the dog for a quick walk outside, Patrick fed and watered the starving dog. His cries were so pitiful that Patrick thought it too cruel to leave him there and decided to take him home. In the morning he would call animal rescue hoping they could find a new home for the ole boy.

Chapter 13
LONELY BOY

The ole scruffy dog with no name, was quickly embraced by Haley and Maura who gave him treats and all the attention he had never received from the Samuels. They decided to give him a name and called him 'Lonely Boy' because the poor dog was just that. Patrick knew that the Samuels were in jail and figured that Jonathan had taken off knowing his friends would probably not be returning. Any pending trial would be years away as the investigators needed to put an airtight case together, circumstantial evidence wouldn't do in the case of a murdered Constable.

As the months wore on Sharon Samuels revealed to the police that the scars on Steven's hands and arms came from a car accident that he caused while trying to commit insurance fraud.

"He rammed into the back of a vehicle belonging to a young couple named Sharon and Steven Samuels. The new Steven aka Cathal McNeal tried to get the couple out of the car and in doing so he burned himself severely. He was able to steal the women's purse and the wallet belonging to the male driver and he even showed compassion for their strange looking unkempt dog.

We then assumed the names of the two that died that day and we were able to use their credit cards and accounts from information found in the women's purse and phone.

The accident occurred late at night on a deserted country road far from the city. Cathal thought it would be the perfect crime and it had been for quite a long while.

The young couple's car burnt to the ground yet somehow, we were able to drive away with minor damage done to Cathal's car except for a dented grill."

"I was shocked at his coldness and realized I was in too deep to just walk away or he would have come after me. I found myself trapped and simply stayed the course, waiting for the opportune time to disappear. Cathal, however, always kept a close eye on me and it was nearly impossible to make an escape from him. I had no money and no job since the drug dealing days with John Stone had come to an end. I was now too old to reinvent myself and wouldn't have known where to start."

As time went on the police found compassion for Melissa aka Sharon knowing how rotten her life was from the poor choices she made through the years. She too, would pay a heavy price in the end but she was at peace with her decision to assist the DA with information that would put Cathal McNeal away forever. For Melissa it was the escape for which she had always wished. She hoped to do her time and be able to walk free one day, if only for a while.

Since most of the mysteries of Constable Harrison's death were in the open and the perpetrators had been caught the police felt a sense of closure with his case.

The latest information given by Ferron regarding where John Stone had spent many years of his life since his Houdini exit from the world were coming to light, giving each of them some peace of mind.

Maura decided that her time with Haley and Patrick must come to an end. Sadly, she made flight reservation to leave the next day, which came too soon. The sound of songbirds happily singing their melodic tunes had awakened the family early. A breakfast surprise awaited Maura as she joined Haley and Patrick on the back patio. Much to her surprise, Ferron and Olivia were present as well, and each bore a gift of thanks to Maura for her courage at coming forth with the information that certainly was heading toward John Stone's arrest, if in fact they could locate him.

Maura kept apologizing for keeping her secret for far too long. She promised to stay connected and perhaps visit again under different circumstances if she could motivate Carl to leave the homestead. Hardy laughter floated away on a breeze as they chuckled at Maura's statement.

Unexpectedly, an Uber came over the hill to take Maura on her journey home. Hugs and kisses were given and a finally wave from the vehicle window sent her on her way.

Olivia and Ferron stayed on reminiscing over the past weeks of the investigation. The murder of James Harrison and all that Jaden Donaldson finally revealed. There was a profound sense of satisfaction and for many reasons. Olivia stepped into the house and returned with a large album filled with photos from the wedding which she had placed carefully in order regarding the wedding events. Together Patrick and Haley sat on the garden bench and took delight in seeing all their guests enjoying the festivities. Not one of them knew that the dead body of Constable Harrison was in attendance. A chill ran up their spines as they cringed at the thought.

"I guess what you don't know won't hurt you." Ferron said.

"Oh! Ferron, stop! Olivia warned. "There's nothing funny about that."

"I'm only kidding dear, lighten up."

Just then the mail carrier arrived sending Patrick to the front door to retrieve whatever was being delivered. He soon returned to the patio and handed over all the bills and some late letters and cards of wedding well wishes to Haley. One large envelope with a return address stared back at Patrick.

"Humm what could this be?"

Patrick fumbled to open the letter which read.

"Dear Patrick Stone,

A gift has been left for you here at Safe Harbor Marina in Vineyard Haven. Someone will be in the office tomorrow at 1:00 pm to assist you. We will hope to see you then."

Safe Haven Marina Staff.

Immediately everyone grabbed their phones and tapped away trying to locate their address.

"I've got it here, 100 Lagoon Pond Road, Vineyard Haven, Mass 02568"

A quick call to the number listed brought no answer.

"I'll have to wait until tomorrow. That is so odd, who would leave me a gift at the Marina? Not unless the guys bought me a jet-ski or a pair of kayaks for me and Haley. We were joking about that the night we all went downtown."

"If that is the case? It looks like Olivia and I will have to buy a pair too. That will be the perfect recreation for us to enjoy as couples." Would you mind if I go with you tomorrow? That's exciting and now my inquisitive side has been aroused." Ferron replied.

"Sure, I'd love the company. What about you two what's on the agenda for tomorrow?"

"I have a doctor's appointment in at 11:00 then Olivia and I planned on lunch in Oak Bluffs. Sorry we can't make it, but I am sure you'll fill us in as soon as you know what is going on. That's exciting Patrick."

"I know it will drive me crazy for the rest of the day."

Lonely Boy began scratching at the door and Haley opened it up letting him out. He was so excited to be in the sunshine he ran around the yard like a fool, then ended up with his head in Haley's lap looking for some loving head rubs. His big brown eyes stared at Haley and her heart melted.

"Patrick, if you don't mind? I'd like to keep him. He is like an extra house alarm with his loud barking. I think I'd feel much more comfortable to know he was here, especially when you are on the mainland. What do you say?"

"Do I have a say in this? He was meant to be here Haley, yes, we will keep him."

"Thank You Patrick. I love you."

"Ferron and I have lots to do at the house since tomorrow is a full day in town. Come on buddy the lawn mower is waiting for you, let's go." Olivia demanded.

"Thanks for a great beginning to the day, it was lovely. I'll miss Maura not being here but at the same time I know you're happy to have your house back. After all you are newlyweds." A smile beamed from Olivia and Ferron as they nodded towards Patrick in agreeance.

The two couples went about their business for the rest of the day. Haley put a call out to her father to see where he had disappeared to.

"We are exploring the island and have been looking at lots of houses. I think we have found the perfect place to buy. Liv and I are staying in

Edgartown tonight and will head home tomorrow afternoon. How is Maura doing? I'm so sorry we didn't spend more time visiting with her."

"She left this morning dad but she promised to come back soon and bring Carl with her."

"Wow, that visit flew by quickly."

"You and Liv were here for the first part of her visit but within the last few days many secrets were discovered about mom and Sam's murders and the whereabouts of John Stone after all these empty years. I'll fill you in when you get home

Chapter 14
SAFE HARBOR MARINA

Saturday morning the doorbell rang at 12 noon sharp. There, stood Ferron with a big grin on his face.

"You ready for the major surprise?" He asked with a chuckle.

"Yep, I can't wait. I don't want to get too excited because it just may be a cruel joke, which, I can't put past some of my buddies."

"Oh, come on, be more positive Pat. If nothing more it will be an adventure."

"I agreed."

With that Ferron decided to be the navigator and plugged the address for Safe Harbor Marina into his phone. Within thirty minutes they pulled into Lagoon Pond Road. The water was a sparkling blue and a light breeze that pushed along Saturday morning novice boaters. Several classes of want to be sailors filled the pond area as sails flapped wildly in the breeze. Colored flags dotted the marina inlet as whopping cheers mixed with bellows from sailing instructors filled the air.

"What a wonderful place to raise kids." Ferron and Patrick said at the same time.

Looking up the hill toward the boat store I saw a rickety old wooden sign that hung on angle which read The Oystered Pearl. At the same time, they saw a middle-aged man unlock the doors and enter inside. Patrick and Ferron followed close behind. In the back corner of the old clapboard building, they found the man on his phone as he rifled through some wrinkled paper files, as he mumbled to someone on the other end. Patrick excused himself as he stuck the letter, he had received under the man nose, stating that someone had left a gift for him. The man hung up the phone quickly and answered Patrick with enthusiasm.

"Oh yes, he said and handed Patrick a wooden board approximately twenty inches long by ten inches high that read. Stone, slip #9. I do have quite a surprise for you. Here, slip # 9 at the end of the dock is yours. Take a right out the door and follow the wooden dock to the end then take a left onto the smaller wooden dock, it's the last slip on the right. You'll want to place this sign on the piling in front of your slip.

Patrick looked toward Ferron with a bewildered expression and shrugged his shoulders.

"Let's go check it out."

With Ferron on his heels, Patrick picked up his pace with a sense of excitement. Within minutes they found themselves looking at a 38-foot older sailing Sloop that shined like new.

"That's my mother's boat, that's 'Samantha's Rig' but where did it come from and who delivered her here? Ferron, please pull up on the bow line so I can view the boat's name on the stern."

Ferron did as he was told and sure enough the boat's name appeared as it had all those years ago. It was 'Samantha's Rig.' A new coat of paint and polished teak on the decking let them know that the boat was totally restored to its original condition. Someone had refurbished her to peak condition spending tons of time and money to do so. But, who and why? What was their interest in doing so? The sails were covered in their protective sleeves, the cleats were shiny and new, the boat lines were pure white having never been used.

Patrick suddenly turned jumped off the boat and ran back up the dock to ask the man in the store who had delivered the boat and when this gift had arrived? Excitedly, Patrick stuck out his hand introducing himself formally.

"My name is Patrick Stone a newlywed, now living on the Island. And You?

"I'm Hank, caretaker of the docks and manager of The Oystered Pearl."

"Can you tell me who brought the boat here? This is a shock! That used to be my mother's boat and I haven't seen her in 20 years."

"She arrived about two weeks ago. She was brought in by an ole sea dog captain who often makes deliveries from the mainland. I only know him by Skip."

"Is he around?"

"No, he never stays here for long. He makes his deliveries and may hit the bars for the night before returning to the other side."

"Were there any messages left for me?"

Hank pulled out a file of paperwork and thumbed through his small mess.

"Here you go, "Enjoy the Rig, it's what she would have wanted." The short message read.

"Skip made arrangements to have new sails, lines, cleats, and the decking refurbished as per the donors' orders. We have taken the liberty of filling the frig with water, wine, food, life jackets and everything you need for a safe sail.

"Who ordered that and who paid for it?"

"He never said, he only followed the directions given and paid in cash."

"I will be here by ten am tomorrow to take her out. I want to tell my wife and see if she willing to come with me. How is the weather forecast for tomorrow?"

"Clear skies and clear sailing, winds at about eight to ten knots. That should be a perfect sailing day." Hank said.

Patrick returned to slip #9 to find Ferron checking out the galley area below, asking if they were going for a sail.

"Not now, but tomorrow morning. Are you coming?"

"I can't. I'm expected to go over to Woods Hole, work is calling for me. Perhaps the four of us can go out over the weekend?"

"That sounds doable. Besides, going alone tomorrow might be the best thing for me because I'm sure I'll have a flood of emotions and bittersweet memories."

The ride back home was mostly in silence as Patrick's mind ran wild wondering who could have sent the boat over to the island.

"Do you think Julieann sent it? Perhaps it was a wedding gift from her, but I'm sure she would have told me at the wedding. No- one really knew where the boat went after mom died and we were in too much misery after mom's death and our years in college to think about what could have happened to the Rig. You don't think this could be from the hand of my father, do you?" Patrick asked.

Ferron sat dumb- founded, not knowing how to respond then added. "Just enjoy someone's kind gesture."

At home Patrick shared his news with Haley who immediately had a million questions most of which, Patrick couldn't answer.

"The Rig looks beautiful. She has been completely done over and is ready for the water. I'm taking her out tomorrow for a brief time. Would you like to join me?"

"Not tomorrow, Pat. I think perhaps it best that you go alone if you think you can manage by yourself. That will be an emotional time for you."

"I just dropped Ferron at home and he suggested maybe we could do a couple's cruise over the weekend. What do you think?"

"Now that's a great idea. You're on Pat."

Patrick suddenly became solemn, retreating to the living room with his mother's diary in hand. He thumbed through the pages as if searching for something specific."

"I on the other hand had quite enough information about my own mother and didn't care to read anymore about her. She in my estimation was evil, a cheat and liar who took advantage of my father's kindness and patience. He had loved her beyond reason and I was unsure of why he kept their relationship going, especially when he knew full well of her infidelities. I had convinced myself that once my dad and Liv settled into their new home that I would take a long walk on the beach with him and ask him directly all the questions I needed to have answered, then, I would be done with it.

It saddened me to think of the happy days we had on Newcomb Drive while my brother and I were in high school. I relished in the memories and all the activities I shared with my parents, because no matter how horrible the things are that I read in my own mother's handwriting. I can't help but fantasize about a dreamier unrealistic truth to her story. How tragic I thought."

After hours Patrick moseyed into the kitchen looking for dinner. I could see that he remained thoughtful but I made chit chat taking him from his inner most thoughts. An early retreat to our bedroom would bring the morning on more quickly. And perhaps a good night's sleep would ease his busy mind.

Chapter 15
DÉJÀ VU

A t dawn, Lonely Boy jumped on the bed as usual, his cries begged Patrick to take him outside for his morning duty and run around the gardens.

It was a glorious day to be filled with a new adventure back on the water. It had been along time since his sailing days in Westport but once you learn how to maneuver a sailboat that knowledge truly never leaves your mind. He had a quick breakfast and sat with Haley for a while before he hit the road for Safe Haven Marina. His excitement sent his belly into a tale spin but he was sure it would settle down with some Pepto Bismol.

Soon, Patrick arrived at slip #9. He went over the boat one last time to check to see that everything was in order and seaworthy, securing a safe sail. He uncovered the sails from their waterproof sleeves, the smell of new canvases filled his nares, spurring several sneezes.

After checking the lower birth area and refrigerator stock, he went up the hill one more time to pick up a few things at The Oystered Pearl, Hank handed Patrick a map of the area and warned of offshore shoals reminding him that at low tide they might give him a challenge. Hank was very helpful and together they walked toward slip #9 and chatted some. Patrick told him that the boat used to belong to his mother who was now deceased. Hank gave his sincere apologies in a reverent voice then offered to give Patrick a hand untying the dock ropes and pushing the Rig from its slip. Thanks were exchanged and Patrick was certain they would become fast friends. A smooth shove from Hank's strong arms sent Patrick on his way. Hank then hollered after Patrick to call him upon his return and he would assist with docking 'Samantha's Rig.'

Surprisingly enough, Patrick remembered all he needed to know for a smooth sail on the 38-footer. He studied the map given to him by Hank so that he would know the lay-out of the sea floor for any sand bars or shoals. It was a glistening day and Patrick certainly felt his mother's presence, occasionally in the whistle of the wind he thought he heard his mother's voice, bringing him to tears. It was then that he raised his head toward the heavens and thanked her for bringing the boat back to him. Patrick promised to keep the Rig in perfect condition for as long as time would allow.

He sailed a good mile from the marina then put the sails down and dropped the anchor allowing the boat to list on the waves. The rhythm of the current and heat of the sun began to make Patrick sleepy. On the aft seating bench, he put his legs up, turned his face toward the sky and puffed up a cushion to rest his head. Soon, his eyes fluttered and his lids rested in a closed position. It wasn't long before dreams of his mother came floating in and old conversations swept through his mind. She was there with him gently rocking to the same rhythm of the waves, bringing back memories long lost in time.

Suddenly, a crash brought Patrick back to reality, he bolted upright trying to find his bearings. His immediate thought went to tides and remembered what Hank said about hidden shoals that could be a problem.

"Hello, hello is anyone there?"

No answer came only the sound of the side buoys banging against the boat. He decided to take the Rig out a bit further as in the distance he could see a small chain of islands within view and thought perhaps that could be his destination for their pending weekend sail with the Michaels.

He pulled the anchor up and listened to the chains clanking as the electronic device did its work. Patrick hoisted the mainsail leaving the jib and genoa secured neatly. Patrick took the wheel and headed in the direction of what seemed to him to be a small chain of islands.

Shockingly, noises came from the lower cabin, a crashing of a fallen dish the shifting of pots and pans, then footsteps ascending the ladder told him that he was not alone.

"Hello who is there? Who is there?" He bellowed with a fearful tremor in his voice.

There he was alone in the middle of the ocean, vulnerable to anyone who may want to harm him. Quickly he wondered if this had been such an innovative idea, to sail by himself.

A moment later a tall figure appeared from the galley area. He was dressed in shorts and a navy-blue hooded sweatshirt; his head was in a downward position. The mystery man then stepped out of the cabin in full view of Patrick. A sudden rocking of the boat set the man's footing off kilter then with a jilted the man stumbled forward landing flat on his face hitting his head hard on the deck. After several minutes, the man lifted his head allowing Patrick to see his face.

"What the hell are you doing here Jonathan? And how dare you infiltrate my private property and my life. What the hell do you want with me? You and those weird neighbor's the Samuels have caused enough disruption in Haley's and my life. I was certain you had left the area. I had looked for you at the Samuels home because the dog whom we've named 'Lonely Boy' was barking for days. Haley and I took him in as our own. Now explain this intrusion and what the hell are you doing here, tell me who you really are.

"It has been a long time Johnny but I thought you would have recognized me or at least remember my voice. I am your father."

Patrick took a long hard stare and still saw no resemblance to the man he knew as his dad nor did his voice have a familiar ring to it.

"I had an accident several years ago that scarred and disfigured me forever."

"Yes, I have only learned of your accident recently, however I have been researching you for some time and finally found out many of your secrets. The first of which is that you lived off the coast of Spain with Nella Michaels for all these years. What the hell do you want with me and why have you come back to haunt us? Don't you think you've done enough damage in this lifetime? You were responsible for the death of two women and the ruin of Julieann and me. I want nothing to do with you.

You treated all of us like strangers as you indulged yourself in whimsical fantasies while making drugs in your personal lab, becoming an addict. How in God's name could you throw your family away? Why did you take mom's life? She was such a beautiful woman and good person. And what about me and Julieann? Were we nothing to you? For God's sake you left us parentless. I hate you for the person you've become. Tell me John, was it worth it to have to hide out and live in another country for all these years?

It truly was a great disguise living off the grid on a faraway island. And to top it off you chose to have a relationship with my friends' aunt and the sister of Jaden Donaldson who happens to be Ferron Michaels father, but of course you already knew that. As word has it, you left Nella high and dry without even a goodbye. I'm sure you have broken her heart as you did ours so long ago. It is unfair and inhumane to hurt people as you do. I know she wonders where you went and why you left. Wonderful job John."

"Look Patrick, I never cared about anyone or anything but my own success and yes, I used anyone and everyone I could to get to where I needed to be and have what I wanted. I know that sounds cruel but my ulterior motives all had to do with money. I knew when I met your mother that she was worth a fortune in stocks and bonds and that one day she would inherit massive amounts of money from her grandfather and spinster aunt.

When we married, she put me on the policies making me the sole beneficiary. It is all that simple. I had to remove her before she thought to add Julieann and your name to the policy, taking away all I had suffered for and what I deserved after all the years of a sexless, dull, boring life with your mother."

"Don't you dare talk about mom in that way. Who do you think you are? You are one fucking bastard lost in your own delusions. Tell me was that the true reason you killed mom, or some sick excuse for your own perversions. And what about Haley's mom? Did you kill her too?"

"That woman was a brainless bitch with an overactive libido. She was an easy mark. I needed her to keep an eye on your mother and we worked out the perfect scenario, having her live with the Morgan's. Two problems under one roof. And yes, I planned with Cathal McNeal to take care of my business. My part in it was to have sex with Maddie and her involvement with Cathal made her collateral damage. She simple knew too much about me and all that was going on."

"I can't believe this."

Rage filled Patrick; his face reddened as if he would explode. Just then the wind kicked up and blew John's shirt into the air. A gun was stuffed into his belt of his shorts and Patrick knew he was there for more than just a conversation.

"Where is Julieann, dad?"

"She is with your mother. I took care of her while she vacationed in Salt Cay in the Turks and Caicos several days ago. I'm sure no one has found her yet."

Patrick let out an anguished scream as he charged his father tackling him to the deck. He and John fought with a sense of ferociousness as Patrick scrambled to take John's gun away. John shot off a right hook smashing Patrick's face quite badly. During his fall to the deck Pat smacked his head on a line cleat. He grabbed his head to stop the pain and felt blood drip from his temple and cheek. Patrick rolled away taking a moment to shake himself back to reality. He stumbled as he got on his feet and move towards the wheel to steady himself. The word disbelief flew through his mind as Patrick's adrenalin was pumping through his veins furiously. Although taken off guard, he found John fairly easy to overpower because he was no longer agile enough to move quickly. Patrick finally was able to disarm the gun from his father, but not without wounding himself badly.

Once John was stable enough to get on his feet, he began moving towards Patrick in a threatening way. He had one hand in his pocket and the other dangled at his side as if wounded.

"Take your hand out of your pocket, I need to see both hands now!" Patrick demanded.

John hesitated at first then lifted his left hand into the air. He then took his other hand out of his pocket revealing a knife with a serrated steel edge that flipped out into position with the hit of a button on the knifes handle. John made jabbing moves toward Patrick wanting to do severe damage to him. Patrick knew without a doubt that his father meant serious business but Pat had the gun. It was a careful game of cat and mouse they both played, but who would make the first move or end this sick confrontation?

Instantaneously, Patrick remembered his mother's version of her near drowning on Golan Lake and thought about doing the unthinkable. John was positioned perfectly mid-section in the boat and, as if rehearsed, I gust of wind caught the luffing sail as

Samantha's soft voice whispered on the wind clearly, over and over again.

"Do it now Patrick and be done with him." Moments later her voice faded into oblivion.

Patrick turned the wheel filling the sail to its fullest then, let it go. The strength of the boom went slamming, into John's head and shoulders sending him flying over the guard rail and into the water. He screamed for help begging for Patrick to send over a life jacket or preserver. Momentarily, Pat thought he should save the bastard yet a very quick after thought provoked him to send the grappling poll over the side instead. It was like Deja vu remembering his mother's horrific experience and the fear she must have felt.

He couldn't save his father after all the pain and anguish he had put the family through, instead he rammed the pole into his gut sinking him into the chilly water, just like Maddie had done to Sam at John's demand. John's arm's flailed topside as he gasped for air, begging for help. Patrick was determined to honor his mother memory and listened to her demanding words. A movie reel played in his mind suspecting his mother to have been in the same horrifying position that now faced the man who killed her.

Having no regrets, Patrick left his father in the freezing water bobbing up and down as he gulped for air and sent out a pathetic sounding calls for help. Patrick then, smoothly turned the boat around without hesitation and headed back to Shore. From the port side of the boat, he flung a red life preserver over the side somewhere near where John was floating. A coldness mixed with anger came over Patrick as he had absolutely no emotions but only felt it was a score settled after way too many years.

Patrick's eyes scoured the coastline looking for people or any motion at all. Then his eyes turned to the ocean to see if any boats were in the area. There was absolutely nothing in sight. He felt a sense of satisfaction knowing that John would die as he had intended Samantha to do so long ago. Patrick refused to give his father another thought. He then focused on Julieann and the situation she was in; he was determined to send his friends and agents to Salt Cay to find his sister and concentrated on getting her home quickly.

A call went out to Hank ten minutes before his arrival in port to secure an easy docking event. Sure enough, Hank was there waving his arms as he directed Patrick into the slip. Pat reached into his pocket and handed Hank a fifty-dollar bill as he whizzed by him.

"Hey kid what happened to your head and hands? There's a lot of blood all over you."

"I know, just a clumsy mistake or two. I'll be fine. I've got to go, sorry to run but thanks for the help, Hank. You saved my life today."

Patrick gave a sheepish smile then jumped onto the dock. He was shocked at what he had done but ran to the car wanting to put the horror of the day behind him. His mind kept repeating where is Julieann? Dear God let her be found.

Chapter 16
SECRETS AND LIES

Patrick could not stop pondering the thought that his self-absorbed father had intentions of killing him. His actions were as horrific as his father's had been but somehow there was no guilt or after thought of his actions. When he arrived at home, he called his best friend and told him to go with another to Salt Cay in search of Julieann as he was with the understanding that she had been injured while on vacation. He gave no other explanation. Patrick would have gone himself but how would he explain the urgency to leave without telling Haley everything and that was not an option.

Haley was curious about what had happened to Patrick's face and the wound on his hand, most especially she wondered who it was that brought the boat over to the island. She asked Patrick to indulge her, however, he told her he had no idea and that Hank the manager at The Oystered Pearl was never told who had gifted the boat to him. Hank simply was given a large amount of money to say nothing and make the delivery.

"Do you think your father had something to do with it?" He lied as he told her he didn't know the answer to her questions.

"I'm just happy to have her boat back with me. Someone took the time to fix her up perfectly. Wait until you see her. Please I can't talk about this anymore I'm worried about Julieann."

Over the next few days Patrick waited with anguished anticipation to hear from his friend Miles and of what he might have found on Salt Cay. At 3 am a calypso ringing of Patrick's phone awakened him, He grabbed the phone on the first ring jumped from the bed and headed downstairs out of Haley's ear shot.

"I have found her Patrick; she was flown to Miami's Jackson Memorial Hospital and was beaten pretty badly but she will recover. They never found the perp."

"Thank God. Please tell her I love her and will come as soon as possible."

"Patrick. Give her a few days she's pretty out of it."

"I will and thanks Miles. What would I do without you?"

In the morning Haley took her cup of coffee along with Lonely Boy out back. The house was filled with a sense of a frenzied aura.

"What's wrong Pat?" She asked as he slipped through the door.

"Nothing, all is well. I sent Miles to the Turk and Caicos where Julieann was vacationing. One of her friends got in touch to tell me she had an accident. She was flown to Miami where she is recovering. I'll head down in a few days and bring her here."

'Why not go now. I'll go with you."

"She's in rough shape and needs some time in the hospital to recover. Not to worry, you have Lonely Boy to take care of, I'll manage this."

Haley asked Patrick what had happened to his head and noticed a large bandage on his hand hiding some kind of wound. Patrick flicked her question off saying he was a careless sailor who got wrapped up in the lines. Not for one minute did she believe him yet said not another word. Haley felt a thickness in the air and an ominous feeling even in the house. Something was awry, she just knew it. Patrick would only give her a look and she backed off not wanting to get involved. For all she knew, it could be a new case on which he was working.

Patrick decided they would keep their date with the Michaels for their proposed weekend sail. He knew it was best not to function as if guilty of anything and keep a sense of normalcy at home and with the Michaels.

Samantha's Rig was waiting for them on Saturday morning and the Rig was all set to go. Patrick noticed that his sails had their sleeves placed over them and assumed it was by Hank's helpful hand. He stopped by The Oystered Pearl to give thanks to his new friend.

"You were in such a hurry I thought I'd give you a hand. Next time think, otherwise you could do damage to your gear. Also, I took the liberty to clean off the blood from the deck. You made quite a mess."

"Gottcha, sorry about that and thanks again for your help."

Patrick asked Hank about the currents that day, hoping not to find a floating body in the ocean, he explained that he wanted to head toward that chain of islands somewhere out there. Hank gave him easy directions then took sail.

The sail was an easy one and Patrick took lead on Hank's suggestions.

The Michaels and Haley brought out the wine, cracking a bottle before they made it to the island where they would picnic and search for hidden treasures.

Patrick's eyes scanned the water in search of a floating body or the sight of a red life preserver. Yet, there was nothing to be found, settling his nervous stomach.

An hour and a half sail took them into one of the islands that began a chain of uninhabitable land formations that formed a barrier reef at one time. He surmised it had at one point been one large plot of land in the middle of the sea eroded with time to make small plots of islands.

Soon they let the anchor down and took the skiff off the back of the boat and loaded themselves and their wares into it. As they headed to shore, they saw a small inviting beach and bushy lush thickets of trees and shrubbery. It was the perfect place for their afternoon adventure.

They polished off several more bottles of wine, ate their lunch while they sun bathed. Then took an adventure scouring the island to see what treasures she held. A towel filled with shells, conches and sea glass was hauled back by the girls for crafts they would make.

Patrick was feeling restless and longing to get back home.

Within a half hour they were back on Samantha's Rig and heading for the marina.

Of course, Patrick was relieved that he saw no remnants of his altercation with his father and he was certainly glad to get the hell out of there.

Once at home. A call was made to Miles for an update on Haley's condition.

"How is she doing?"

"She is coming along but her concussion has left her a bit loopy. The doctor said to give her to the end of the week. Apparently, a man has attempted to visit her here. I have put a no visitation on her."

"Who was it, do you know?"

"No, I don't, but I was told by hospital staff that he is an older well-dressed, handsome man of color."

"I'll head down soon. Send me the name of your hotel or just go ahead and book a reservation for me. Two days from now is good."

"You've got It." See you then."

It was smooth flying from Boston into Miami on Delta airlines. Miles picked up Patrick and took him directly to the hospital. It was obvious that his nerves were on edge anticipating how Julieann would look. She was sitting up in bed and although bruised and banged up pretty good she was cognitive and speaking rationally.

Miles had waited for Patrick before beginning with a slew of questions.

"Did you see who did this to you."

"No, he attacked from behind, all I saw was a long smooth black man's arm reach around my middle. I was hit on the back of my head several times, which knocked me out. I felt several kicks to my ribs and decided it best to laid on the floor pretending to be dead when a voice said. "That's enough. she is dead."

"But Mr. Donaldson one more whack should do her in for sure. Come on we have to complete the job. I think she's still alive."

"Leave her be, she will either die soon or at least she got the message."

"Our contract was to make sure she was dead. Sir."

"I said forget it, enough is enough."

"The two men left me lying in a pool of blood and only semi-conscious. A time later I was found by room service as I had ordered dinner to my room. I guess you could say I was lucky."

Immediately, Patrick's mind floated back to Martha's Vineyard and the Michaels, knowing Ferron's father was involved and present at the attack. It was unsettling but seemingly, Jaden saved her life at the same time. He put out a call to Haley warning her to keep to herself until he arrived back home. He cautioned her to keep away from the Michaels fearing they may do something unconscionable to Haley. She understood and made him feel at ease.

Patrick couldn't wait to confront Ferron upon his return and hunt down Jaden Donaldson. After all he was the man who made money by doing others' dirty work. It all stemmed from my father's hiring of him to take care of his personal business.

It took several more days before they could leave for Boston. The ride was smooth and Julieann had an uneventful flight and grateful to be back on the Vineyard.

The next day Patrick made arrangements for the Michaels to stop by for dinner and to spend time with Julieann. After dinner they sat around the fire pit in the garden area enjoying a drink when suddenly Ferron looked up at Patrick and said.

"Brother that whack of your face could have killed you, one more whack would have done you in and look at your hand you're still wearing a bloody bandage."

Suddenly, Julieann took a closer look at Ferron's smooth hairless arms and turned as white as a sheet. She began choking and excused herself so that she might catch her breath away from the others. Patrick followed her inside and asked if she was okay.

"No, I'm not okay. Patrick that is the same voice of the guy that attacked me at the hotel."

"Are you sure about that? You can't just accuse someone because you think so or because he is black."

"I know that Patrick, I'm not dumb, I'm telling you he is the one that attacked me. His voice has the same cadence and tambour. It is the same man."

There was no way that Patrick could confront Ferron right then. He made an excuse to his company telling them that Julieann was tired and needed to go to bed early.

The Michaels understood and bid their adieus.

"I'll see you tomorrow, Ferron. We need to chat." Patrick's voice had a commanding tone to it, setting off alarms in Ferron's mind.

Haley and Patrick then nestled onto the couch and turned on the late news to hear Ryan Kristafer, commentator on the island news station, reveal that the body of a man had floated up on Devil's Island at the farthest end of the barrier island chain.

"An unknown boater's attention was drawn to a red floating life vest with no one attached to it. The man was horrified when he pulled his boat onto the island for further investigation. He stated that a dead person was swollen from being in the sea for some length of time and looked to be mutilated, from what was seen by him and rescue personnel. The man's face and hands had been severely burnt, leaving no way to identity him. His tattered clothing revealed no drivers license or other forms of identification on his person. It is thought that his boat caught fire, sinking the vessel. We will have more details after the coroner's report and a sonar search of the immediate area, as they look for the sunken vessel." Ryan said.

Early the next morning, Patrick called the Vineyard police to report what Julieann had told him about her attack and near death. They said they would send someone out to the house. In the meanwhile, Patrick went to the Michael's home. There was no answer at the door and both vehicles were gone. All the shades were pulled, which was not like Olivia to do so. Suspicious! Patrick thought. He tried both cell phones but neither were being answered. He tried to GPS the phone's location but they were both turned off. A call to the Ferry in Oak Bluffs revealed that the Michaels had left the island on the ten o'clock ferry the night before.

Immediately, Patrick attempted to reach Jaden Donaldson, but had the same results, absolutely nothing!

An expeditious search was implemented of all airlines out of the Boston area. It quickly revealed that three reservations were made two days after Julieann arrived back on the vineyard for two men and one woman of color which was revealed by their passports. No doubt these individuals could have been anyone, however, the timing was too coincidental not only that but the agents recovered photos of their passports affirming they were the Michael's and Mr. Donaldson.

Patrick and Haley knew then that it was a set-up. Their entire friendship with the Michaels was nothing more than a fraud and scam. The Michaels instrumented everything that happened on the island including the carnage in the gardens, the dumping of Harrisons body and removal of his vehicle. They too were suspect in the attack of Julieann in the Turks and Cacaos and everything that went on at the Vineyard since their move to the island, including the deposit of Samantha's Rig at the marina. They were now suspects and would be prosecuted for Constable Harrison's death. Ferron and Olivia were such great actor's and we were so fooled by them. Even Olivia's beating by Steven was nothing more than a lie. She was an active part in the entire scheme, seeming to enjoy her stellar deception and raw vagrancy of the sick relationship they conjured up with the Stones.

Haley and Patrick were both stunned and as angry as hell to think they were such poor judges of character. It was absolutely humiliating to realize that their own naivety was unequivocally mind-blowing. With all their education in the field of law they should have known better and should have questioned the pushiness of the Michaels, yet the newlyweds were anxious to make new friends on the island and were drawn in by Olivia and Ferron's seeming friendliness and caring attitudes.

Eventually, the Michaels would be brought to justice if ever found in that vast sea of people living in Europe and beyond all borders.

"The manhunt was on."

CPSIA information can be obtained
at www.ICGtesting.com
Printed in the USA
BVHW030827141122
651891BV00019B/522/J